GLAM

To

Assunta.

I hope you enjoy this book and read it it over and over again.

Love

Dave

Lawson.

xxxx

Diana Lainson

GLAM & GLITZ

The Heartfelt Press

A HEARTFELT PRESS PAPERBACK

ISBN: 978 1 78695 202 8

THE HEARTFELT PRESS
is an imprint of
Fiction4All

Published 2019

"Beneath the glam and glitz there is

sorrow and intrigue"

PROLOGUE

Fabiana pulled her long dark hair into a ponytail before applying her makeup and smoothing moisturiser on her lovely face as she looked carefully at her translucent skin in the large mirror in front of her. It was so different to what she'd looked like when she was a teenager.

She glanced at her diamond Rolex watch on her left wrist which had been a gift from Antonio when she was twenty two at her coming out party and she always wore it. It would be one hour and twenty minutes until the limousine arrived.

In about six months' time this high pressure life style would be over. How glad she would be. Modelling had been very good to her, but only ever as a means to an end. At this moment in time, she was still the face of Donnetti, but soon she would own the entire company and all that went with it. She would most likely hand it over to her new managers she had chosen and then she could semi-retire and be a proper mother.

She stared dispassionately at the beautiful face in the mirror that had looked out from countless magazines and newspapers and been admired on the World's most famous catwalks for nearly twenty five years, a face envied all over the world by millions of women and adored by men.

When she had begun modelling all those years ago at the age of twenty two, she had been a worldwide trendsetter with her dramatic bone structure, her café-au-lait coloured Latin American skin, her turquoise eyes, waist length wavy black hair and her height of six foot two in bare feet. It was the right look at the right time and she owed it all to her guardian, Antonio Donnetti, who had adopted her and taken her out of Columbia and shown her a completely new life.

She conjured up in her mind a picture of Antonio. He was thirty eight years old when she first met him and her name then was Maria Emelia Ferrero. She lived in abject poverty and misery in Bogota, Columbia until she was twenty when her life changed dramatically and later her rise to fame all over the World as a renowned model, known as FABIANA.

Now nearly twenty five years later she was in London staying at her favourite hotel -The London Savoy, in the Strand - waiting for her limousine to arrive to take her to London Airport to board a plane bound for Paris France, there she would meet up with her ex-husband, Tristan, at Charles de Gaulle airport and they would fly on to Lyon-Saint-Exupéry International Airport and then travel by limousine to where the funeral of Antonio would take place at the Basilica of Notre-dame de Fourvière.

BOOK ONE
CHAPTER ONE
MEMORIES

The last time Fabiana had seen Antonio alive was just over six months ago when he phoned her and they met at the private clinic in Switzerland for the last time when he told her he had been diagnosed with terminal cancer.

Antonio had come to her wedding to give her away when she was nearly twenty nine to see her marry one of the most famous and richest men in the world, Tristan Eves, once a very famous rock star, now the owner of a chain of extremely successful nightclubs in America and Europe and also the biggest recording company in the World - ***Eves Entertainment*** - his latest acquisition.

After two years of being married to Tristan she found out he was gay and she also found about the stream of young men that Tristan had indulged in during their time together before they were married. That of course had been a very a well-kept secret from the media. His agent made sure that he was always surrounded by beautiful young women for any shoot that he participated in, but she didn't really care, she was going to have the one thing she most wanted in her life, a child.

At last, a child of her own sired by the one man in her life that she had always really loved. In a few months' time her high-pressure life style would be over, she was expecting a baby after a year of IVF and was now pregnant. How glad she was. Modelling and everything that went with it had been very good to her, but only as a means to an end.

Once more she glanced at herself in the full-length mirror and patted her slight bump. She looked stunning in the elegant black silk Donnetti outfit that had been especially designed for her.

She glanced again at the small diamond watch on her left wrist. In approximately ten minutes the limousine would arrive at the hotel and whisk her away to Heathrow International Airport and then onto France, where she would meet up with her ex-husband, Tristan who had made up their differences, over the years.

They would make their way to the Basilica of Notre-Dame de Fourvière. She picked up her wide brimmed black veiled hat and black handbag and left her hotel room closing the door quietly and then walked quickly through the plush corridor of the Savoy towards the lift and pressed the button on the wall. Her luggage was already waiting for her in the foyer of the hotel.

***

The cortège came to a halt outside of the beautiful Cathedral in the town of Lyon, France.

Fabiana's ex-husband, Tristan, in his made to measure black suit, black silk shirt and black crocodile shoes, stepped out of the leading funeral limousine and smiled at her as he took hold of her left arm. He thought how beautiful she looked and a lump came in his throat as he guided her up the steps of the great building. Motherhood would suit her he knew. He still loved her in his own strange way and they still kept in touch after they divorced.

They were followed by their two bodyguards and just a few of Antonio's close friends and some of the models he had made famous over the years. Several of the French paparazzi were hovering around along with two from Italy and America and three from England.

As they entered the great building a tall priest came forward and shook their hands and led them down to an empty pew at the front of the church facing the altar and coffin.

As they walked down the aisle Fabiana could hear the strains of one of Antonio's favourite pieces of music - *La Cathédrale Engloutie by Claude Debussy*…(The Sunken Cathedral), being piped through the Cathedral.

Fabiana paused and looked into the carved wooden, open coffin before they took their seats in the front pew. She noticed Antonio's shoulder length black hair had been combed back off his face and she hardly recognised him. His face was gaunt and grey looking and he looked so old. She held back her tears and turned away.

Antonio's open coffin, lined with white satin, had already been placed on a *catafalque…(a decorated wooden frame supporting the coffin of a distinguished deceased person),* in front of the impressive altar and it was surrounded with white Arum Lilies and red and yellow roses with gypsophilia and asparagus fern draping elegantly over the sides of it.

Fabiana had chosen the flowers that he had loved so much. She remembered that he always had an abundance of flowers everywhere in his homes in different parts of the World.

The service was conducted by the Bishop of Lyon, and the prayers read by the resident priest. There was only one hymn, *Jesu, Dulcis Memoria*…(Jesus the very thought of you)…a very celebrated 12th century hymn.

Fabiana had followed Antonio's instructions for his funeral which he had arranged some months before he died, with his Advocate in France.

Antonio's close friend, Dr Martinez, from Columbia gave the address and spoke about Antonio's life and how much he would be missed by Fabiana, himself, his close friends and of course by those in the fashion world.

Behind her, Fabiana heard several of the young, as well as older models weeping. She had no tears left. She had wept in private and was determined to keep a strong face, but, her heart was broken. Antonio had been like a father to her as well as her confidant and later in life her lover and business partner.

***

After the blessing, Fabiana once more took the arm of her ex-husband and followed the pallbearers as they carried the closed coffin out of the Cathedral and towards the burial plot in the large old cemetery of the church.

"*Cendres aux cendres et de la pousière à la pousière*"...(ashes to ashes and dust to dust), intoned the Bishop in French as he made the sign of the cross and two of the altar boys waved their incense burners over the closed heavy oak casket being lowered into the ground.

Fabiana looked down seriously as the coffin was lowered into the ground and threw three red roses on top of it. A little silent prayer passed over her lips and she crossed herself. She knew that Antonio would always be by her side watching and guiding her. She believed in the hereafter as he had. She knew she would write her book now, Antonio had told her so many times in the past to do so. Now she belonged to no one, only herself and the child who was growing inside of her.

The small sad crowd also came forward and looked down at the coffin in the gaping hole, paying their respects. One of the French paparazzi pushed his way forward and took several shots of the grave and the mourners and especially Fabiana.

As Fabiana looked down into the grave she felt a slight stirring of the child inside of her and she placed a protective hand on her stomach and smiled knowing that she was safe now.

After the Bishop had made the sign of the cross again, she turned and walked away from the grave and stood on the river bank and looked down at the small stream that was running through the cemetery.

One cannot go back in life, one has to go forward and that is what she had done, she told herself as she walked slowly back to the graveside to join Tristan and the other mourners.

The gravediggers had started to shovel sods of earth on top of Antonio's coffin. There was also a small Bobcat nearby ready to smooth out the surface of the earth on the grave ready for the headstone to be placed at a later date.

Fabiana had made all the arrangements and would return to Lyon shortly after her child was born to check that the funeral directors had dressed the grave properly according to her instructions.

Tristan her ex-husband led her back slowly to the waiting limousine that would take them back to his private aeroplane at Lyon, but not before stopping at Antonio's solicitor's office in Lyon for an hour or two. Antonio's advocate had mentioned something about a will and properties to Fabiana.

She leaned back into the comfortable rear seat of the large black funeral limousine and thought about her past.

When did her story really begin?

BOOK TWO
CHAPTER TWO
FABIANA'S NEW LIFE

Fabiana had been baptised with the name of Maria Emilia Ferrero. She came from a very poor family in the slum area of Bogotá, Columbia, where violence, drug abuse and prostitution were commonplace. Carlos Emilio Ferrero her father, was dead. He was caught up in a fight, relating to drugs, ten years before.

Her alcoholic and drug taking mother, Laura Maria Morales was left to bring up the four children, two boys and two girls.

They were lucky, the little house in the shantytown of Bogotá consisted of three rooms. Her mother's small bedroom was a dingy living room, with a small kitchen area with cold running water where they cooked and also washed themselves. The other was a bedroom, in which she and her sister had shared with their brothers for a while. But it was no longer divided in half with a long torn and frayed curtain as it was before, when her father had been alive.

Sometime ago her brothers Julio and Carlos had left, having found some menial work in the next village and stayed with their uncle Jaime in another town.

There was also an outside toilet with a water tap and a bucket that they shared with their next-door neighbour. They were one of the lucky few to even have some running water, as most of the women got their water from an old well half a kilometre away in the centre of the town. The water though was often polluted and had to be boiled to stop disease spreading.

When Maria was eighteen and a half years of age she made two big decisions. One, she was going to leave the poor town and second she was going to be a famous model and call herself, Amelia or Fabiana, just like one of the models in the pictures of the magazines which she had retrieved from the rubbish dump in the small town. She had poured over them many times and then hidden them away under her old mattress in case her mother found them and threw them away.

Fabiana was also the name of one of her heroines in two American paperbacks that she had also managed to salvage from the tip and she had hidden them as well.

They were written in English, but she painstakingly with the help of an old English/Spanish dictionary, had translated the stories even though some of the pages were missing, but they had cover pictures that were fading from age. One was a love story and the other a thriller and the beautiful Fabiana was the heroine in one of the books. In the end she decided that the name ***FABIANA*** was the most romantic name.

The second decision was that if she could not be a model, she would one day, when she was older go to America and find a job and marry a nice young American man and raise a family.

Her English, even though quite poor, having left the Mission school when she was sixteen years old to look after her alcoholic mother and run things at home, had not stopped her studying at home. She was a very bright girl and she quickly picked up the language from the books and also from the small 12" black and white TV they had in their meagre house when she watched American soap operas and films.

Her sister, Marissa, who was six years older than her, had for the last four years made a little money cleaning at the local brothel and sometimes selling her body, but the money nearly always ended up in the hands of their mother to buy cigarettes, drink or drugs. Sometimes her sister managed to keep a few centavos for herself and give a few to her younger sister. Maria vowed she would never resort to selling her body, unless it was for a lot of money, but eventually she had no option.

When Maria was twenty, her sister introduced her to her pimp - Marco. No one seemed to know his surname, he was just known as Marco the Supplier. He ran a rundown brothel on the outskirts of their town. Marco's so called office where he operated from, was one of eight rooms that were on the ground floor of the long low building.

Marco realised that soon Maria would be old enough to work for him as one of his girls, but in the meantime she could be trained as a prostitute and also work in the brothel cleaning and running messages for him.

There was one room at the top of the building where he conducted his business with his clients, peddling in drugs and human flesh and undertaking the odd contract for certain people. The room was quite big and the water from the leaking roof in the rainy season only dripped in one corner. There was even a toilet that was shared with four other rooms from the first floor, but at least it had a door.

The first two floors of the dilapidated building were not so bad, they were a bit better than the rotting attic in the roof that consisted of four small rooms which also let the rain in during the rainy season. The attic rooms were where the new young women and young men were trained to prostitution and then later moved down to the second or first floor to entertain their customers.

The entrance hall of the brothel where the old Madame and some of the girls sat on show had a small desk with an old black and white 12" TV and two lumpy red leather sofas. The Madame, who was named Teresa, was in charge of the girls and handed out the condoms and advice but, Marco was ever present to take the money, because he trusted no one.

When Maria first set eyes on the room in the attic, she understood immediately why it was called The Bad Room. It looked like a prison cell.

It was a small room with a narrow bed against the wall on the left. The bed had no headboard it was just a mattress on a rusty metal frame. Beside it was a bare little white bedside cabinet, with no front to it and the paint was peeling off it. There were also little spiders living in it. On the cabinet was an old brass kerosene lamp with a cracked red glass globe that glowed weakly. There was no door only an old red velvet curtain covering the entrance.

The walls of the sleazy room were dark grey and there were no windows or mirrors. To the right was a small doorway to the meagre bathroom with a tiled floor, an old toilet without a cover, a grubby cracked porcelain wash-hand basin and an equally grubby bidet. Maria noticed that the fixtures on it were rusted and rotten. It had been sometime since water had actually run into it she thought.

Looking around the horrid room, she sensed some of the terror and sadness others must have felt locked up in it and forced to stay in such a hovel, with no sunlight, no air, nothing but dark walls to stare at. The room felt evil.

Sighing she threw off her clothes, leaving them in a scrambled heap onto the floor as she turned off the kerosene lamp and crawled bone-tired and aching into her bed. She blushed a little suspecting that the drink Marco had given her was causing the floating effect, she wondered if he was going to visit her that evening and she would get more training.

He would sample his merchandise before he used them for his evil deeds and some of them, the older ones, were hooked on crack or whatever was their habit and very rarely had any money of their own to spend after he had taken his share from them.

Maria's professional name given to her by Marco was Little Maria and after two weeks he moved her from the attic to the first floor as she attracted a lot of business for him. He was careful at first not to introduce her to any hard drugs as she was his youngest girl and he slowly trained her over six months. She in due course became besotted by him and obeyed his every wish, unaware that he was controlling her. She worked in the brothel, cleaning up, cooking if needs be, coffee for some of Marco's, running messages for some of his clients and the Madame also over the months. She hardly saw her drunken mother who was becoming more and more greedy for her heroin.

The room that Little Maria was in was on the ground floor, which his regular paying customers used and she often gave them coffee whilst they were waiting. They were not quite as bad as the others and at least they were cleaned twice a week by an old lady from the village as well as Maria.

Maria listened from her dividing wall and there came unmistakable sounds of violence. Originally it had been a big room, but like the other three rooms, had been divided with plasterboard walls making eight small rooms in all with a corridor that led from the entrance hall to the rooms and also to the back of the old house, where several of the special customers came in, not wanting to be seen entering by the front door.

Maria curled herself into a ball and listened to the noises penetrating the thin wall.

"No," It was a new girl's voice sobbing and distraught.

"Please not again, no, not again."

There was a sudden crash and then another. The girl cried out again and then there was silence. Maria pulled the old sheet over her head and tried to go to sleep.

***

Little Maria was now just twenty one, but she looked younger and she was waiting for her first client that day and she was so exhausted from her other chores.

She had been moved to another room yet again, this time with a door and was dressed in a very short thin white dress and tiny white frilly panties and high-heeled red imitation patent mules with a fluffy pompom on the front. Her long dark hair was parted in the middle and pulled off her face and plaited and tied at the ends with two red ribbons. The Madame of the brothel had powdered her face a little, added some blusher and put just a touch of red lipstick on her full lips and she looked like a doll.

The man who requested her was in his late fifties and usually he did not want penetration with the other girls, just hand relief or a blow-job, as he could not always get it up in his alcoholic state. Little Maria used to walk around the room and slowly undress and display her naked body to him.

He would touch her and caress his penis through his trousers at the same time trying to make it erect and then push her head downwards until she was kneeling on the floor. She would then pull at his trousers, throw them to one side and take his tiny member in her mouth. He would groan whilst she gave him a blow job and he would ejaculate into her mouth, forcing her to swallow it.

The first time when she had done what he wanted her to do, she was almost sick as she gagged on his acrid smelling ejaculation, but she soon learnt to spit it out as soon as he turned his back on her and pretend that she had enjoyed it. Marco had told her to be nice to the ugly old man as he was such a good client and there would be more money for her. More like for him she thought.

But today he wanted penetration with her, without a condom. He bragged to her that Marco had sold him a Viagra tablet and he was ready for her.

She told him that it was forbidden without a condom to have his way with her, also there would be no penetration, Marco had told her, the man but had been drinking a lot and was in a violent mood. She did not want him taking his wrath out on her and be his battering-ram like his wife had been for so many years.

He offered her some cheap brandy from a bottle that he had smuggled into the brothel. For fear of antagonising him she took the bottle and had a gulp of the fiery liquid and handed it back to him. She could feel it racing through her body, she never drank alcohol, but this was an exception and also a bit of Dutch courage for her.

The ugly man also told her his wife had walked out on him two days before, taking their teenage children with her and he was obviously in a bad mood. Maria knew it was because he was violent and she'd probably had enough. She often wondered if he had abused his own daughters in the same way, as she knew that his pubescent girls had been taken into care by the authorities some months before and were living in the Convent outside of the town.

He swayed before Maria and grabbed her and pushed her down onto the small hard bed in one corner of the depressing room and pulled her dress from her, tearing the thin white material and then tore her little white knickers off. She screamed with fear as he broke her virginity.

The drunken man held her down, face up and quickly entered her and within seconds he had ejaculated into her. He then shouted out for her to turn over as he was still hard and he roughly forced himself into her again. This time into her virgin anus, the pain was excruciating and she screamed out aloud, she had never been taken before that way.

Her client staggered again, the vast quantity of alcohol he had consumed together with the Viagra was taking its toll as he withdrew himself from her and fell back on the bed, he was breathing heavily and she thought he was going to pass out as he was so still.

Maria stood up and looked down at the disgusting old man and thought that she could easily kill him with something heavy and she kicked out at one of his legs hanging over the bed. He still did not move, she wondered if he'd had a heart attack.

She looked around her and picked up the heavy brass kerosene lamp that was alight and flickering standing in one corner of the room on a small table. It was the only weapon that she could find in the room and she brought it down with as much force as she could and hit him on the head but it caught him on the side of his face instead.

He fell to the floor together with the lamp that burst into big flames as the cracked glass globe broke into several pieces, burning the man's hair and some of the kerosene seeped out onto the floor and the flame followed the stream of liquid and the small tattered rug on the floor also burst into flames.

The man stumbled towards her as she backed away from him closer to the door, closer to freedom, but afraid to make the final dash that would bring her within the reach of his brutal hands.

Her left breast was exposed by her torn dress.

He lunged at her again and then he swayed from side to side but the vast amount of alcohol that he had consumed had taken its toll and he was breathing heavily.

She stepped out of his way, if only she had something heavier to hit him with she thought.

She quickly trod out the flames around with her red mules, but not before the heat from the flames singed some of her hair and burnt her left cheek badly.

She too screamed out with the agony of her burns and listened for footsteps in the hallway, but the people in the brothel were used to screams coming from the bedrooms and took no notice she thought as she wondered if the disgusting man was dead this time.

Reaching down to the floor she retrieved her torn dress and stumbled across the bedroom, dragging her own pain and soreness with her. She had been *abused*. She'd heard the word whispered and read it in forbidden writings beneath the sheets with an old torch she had been given by her sister. But to her, it was filthy, and such a disgrace.

She burst into tears, this was the end of her life, the end of all of her dreams. Who would want her now?

Who would smile as she was led up to the altar on her wedding day? The fiery pain between her legs made walking an agony. Her burnt cheek was throbbing with pain, she wanted to die, quite simply to crumple in the gutter and kill herself.

Suddenly she heard a movement behind her and the man had somehow come round, the flames which had burnt his face and some of his hair, had at last gone out and he reached out for her again, but he was obviously in a lot of pain and too weak to stand up and grab her. She finally reached the door and let herself out and quietly escaped through the back entrance of the brothel.

Maria knew that Marco would be furious with her for the damage she had caused and for upsetting one of his best clients. She was determined that she would never go back to the brothel even if he did come and find her.

***

A small light gleamed through the thin tattered curtains of her mother's house as she slowly approached it. She would try and sneak in, most likely her mother was asleep from the booze or drugs she'd taken and would not wake up.

As she lay back on her old bed at her mother's house, some resemblance of reality was returning to her. The shock of what had happened had cleared her brain of the effects of the unaccustomed alcohol, but she felt nauseous with the pain of the lower part of her body and especially her burnt cheek and she burst into tears, wondering what she was going to do in the future.

***

Little Maria remembered very little over the next five days. Her mother did not disturb her, thinking she'd caught some virus and left her alone. She was still in pain, but it was gradually subsiding. She struggled from her bed, and walked slowly over to the old cracked mirror that was on the bedroom wall. The throbbing had not gone from between her legs though.

As Maria looked at herself in the speckled mirror she noticed that her face was thinner and paler than usual and the skin on her cheek was red raw. She knew that she would be scarred for life. She was so afraid and burst into tears. What would happen to her now, who could she turn to now?

***

So far Marco had not returned from his long business trip, as he called it. He always did this when something special cropped up, he could be gone for several months. Madame Teresa at the brothel told her, that was the reason that he had not gone to her house to find her, but Maria lived in fear of his wrath if he did.

That was the least of Maria's worries, she knew she was pregnant and didn't know what to do. Her sister had left home and gone off with her pimp from another town several kilometres away and did not want to be contacted.

Her drunken mother would be of no help, she wasn't aware what time of the day it was, as long as she had her drink, drugs and cigarettes she just lolled around now that she had lost her cleaning job with an Italian family and what little money that her sister had left behind was dwindling away sadly.

Maria knew a little about births, she had read the Bible and Mary and Joseph's story and the young girl living down the road had got pregnant when she was abused by her father, but somehow they had got rid of the baby.

She had visited the small library attached to the church in the town and looked in the books of health, the ones with pictures and knew that an unwanted baby could be removed, like a nasty tumour could be cut out.

She remembered that her aunt the year before had been to the local hospital and had a growth taken away from inside of her and the doctors had also cut one breast off. But she couldn't approach her and explain as she knew that her aunt did not want anything to do with her sister or any of her family.

That's what she needed someone to take the baby out of her. But Maria knew that it was nearly impossible, being a devout Catholic, she knew it was also a mortal sin. She had not been to confession for a long time, she was afraid to tell the priest that she might be having a baby, but it was not her fault.

The horrible man at the brothel who had attacked her, had at least been paid back for the ugly deed and had also been badly burnt in the fire that she had caused and later moved away from her town.

Maria had so many sins to confess, she didn't know what to do! She knew that she would have to eventually tell her mother, but what good would that do?

After nearly three and a half months of many tears and indecision Maria went back to the brothel. Where else could she go? She needed money for her mother's habit.

Marco had returned and took her back without any explanation or hesitation; he knew he could still make a lot of money out of her even though she was scarred. But she had not told him that she might be pregnant.

She was left with a large red scar on her left cheek that was pitted from the flames, but he told her to put some heavy makeup on it and pull her long hair over to hide it and also to make sure that the lighting in the rooms were very low. He knew his customers didn't care anyway; they rarely looked at the girls' faces.

Fortunately even though she was tall, she was still very thin looking and her clothes still fitted, even when the books she'd read said they wouldn't. The rounding of her small breasts she assumed was all part of puberty, not that they were much bigger, no one had really noticed except perhaps one or two of her clients. But she knew that she must do something about her dilemma before it was too late, otherwise she would never be able to escape the poverty that she had been brought up in.

CHAPTER THREE
MARIA'S DILEMMA

"Mama, I must speak to you." Maria begged as she stood near the old square sink in the kitchen feeling faint.

She splashed cold water on her face, then hung over the sink wondering if she was going to be sick again. She felt nauseated and very afraid, her emotions were so tangled she had an overwhelming desire to run out of the room and go and hide somewhere.

The water she drank from her cupped hands seemed to calm her stomach and she dried herself with a towel before turning her attention to her drunken mother.

As usual her mother was laying down on the dirty old ragged settee covered with an old patched-work throw-over in the kitchen area, watching an old black and white American TV soap with sub-titles in Spanish.

"Mama, I need to speak to you." Maria and walked over to the TV and shut it off.

"Did you hear me Mama?" She shouted again at her mother.

Her mother smelt of booze and cigarettes and cheap scent that had been on too long to cover the smell of her sweat and urine and Maria gagged as she sat down on the end of the filthy settee next to her.

"What do you want now?" Her mother slurred, not really interested in her young daughter.

"I have not had my bleedings for about five months, Mama, what shall I do?"

Her mother raised herself slowly to a sitting position, grunting and groaning. She remembered that her daughter had been sick on a couple of occasions, but she thought that it had been food poisoning from the fish that they sometimes were able to obtain, even though it had been a bit smelly, they'd eaten it. Now this! What was she to do?

"You slut, you've gone and got yourself pregnant with that pimp of yours, I suppose. Get out, don't tell me, tell that pimp, ask him to help you." She shouted at her as she reached for the almost empty bottle of Tequila on the floor beside her and raised it to her lips.

Maria knew that her drunken mother would be of no help to her at all now and she burst into tears; she knew that if she told Marco, he would probably hit her or throw her out of the brothel. Fortunately he was away again on business and not due back for at least three more weeks.

She had told the Madame that her mother was sick and she had to look after her and was only able to work part-time for a while. She knew that her sister would probably help her but she did not know how to reach her because she had left home and gone to the City.

Maria knew enough by now that she desperately needed to find someone else to help her so she decided finally to go back to the brothel and ask Madame Teresa to help her.

"You stupid young woman." The woman said. "You are supposed to take precautions, you know the rules here, you have been supplied with condoms. Marco will not be best pleased when he returns next week, something has to be done. How far gone are you? "

"I have now missed five bleedings. But, it was not my fault, at first I thought it was Marco's, but he was always careful. You know I was deflowered by that terrible man, you remember, the one who caused the fire and the burn on my face, and what was I to do? He refused to use a condom. He hit me and threw me to the floor and held me down, don't you remember? The fire! Don't you understand? He forced me to have sex with him, he was the cause of all this. Look at my face, I will have this scar forever, what am I to do?" She sobbed loudly.

The old lady looked at the young girl and suddenly felt a wave of pity for her, she too had once been in a similar situation, but her mother had helped her and she had been taken to a woman who dealt with such things. She knew there was a similar person just outside of the town. But she knew, the girl had hardly any money.

"Let me think about it for a couple of days. I might be able to help you. When Marco returns next week, I will tell him that you are still sick and need some more time off. I will send one of the girls to fetch you when I have set it up. I will try to go and see a person who might be able to help you. By the way when we visit her bring a bunch of flowers, and then the neighbours will think you are my friend and we are just visiting the woman."

She handed Maria some centavos to buy the flowers as she knew the young woman did not have much money.

The Madame doubted whether the old woman would be able to do anything as it would soon be too dangerous for the young woman. She also knew that the neighbours of the woman knew exactly what went on in her house and she smiled inwardly with contempt for her.

***

It was a small dark house, with dirty curtains in the windows, and the look of the aged woman who opened the door made Maria shudder. But the Madame promised it would be over quickly and done well.

Maria had brought the flowers as requested and all of her meagre savings with her and hoped she had enough money. She had been horrified when she'd been told how much it would cost.

The old woman who called herself a nurse, asked her a series of questions. She wanted to make sure that the foetus hadn't gone too far, and after taking her money, she led Maria into a small, shabby bedroom at the back of the house.

There was a narrow couch in the middle of the dingy room. The sheets and blankets looked dirty, and there were dry bloodstains on the floor that no one had bothered to clean up after the last visitor had come to see the so called *nurse*.

"Get up on the couch, I must examine you first."

The old aged woman washed her hands in a bowl of water standing in one corner and she took out a tray of instruments which had just been sterilised, or so she said, from a cupboard against the wall, but they looked dirty and terrifying to Maria, as she turned her head away from the sight of the old woman and closed her eyes, breathing deeply as she felt sick with fear.

"My father was a doctor and I was his nurse before he died." Explained the woman, but Maria didn't want to hear about it, she just wanted to get it over and done with and leave the dingy place.

The woman told her to take most of her clothes off and Maria's hands trembled uncontrollably as she did so. Finally she lay on the filthy plastic covered examination couch wearing only her brassiere, with her knees up and her legs open, as the woman examined her and nodded her head. The nurse could feel the tight lump low in the girl's belly.

"You are a good way along, you should have come sooner, but I will do what I can." She said as she pushed hard on Maria's stomach with two fingers pressed into her flesh until she started to wriggle, then the woman examined her inside and poked around.

Nothing that had so far happened in Maria's life, had prepared her for this humiliation, horror and pain. She began to cry with fear and then vomited.

"Let's get started then." The nurse said firmly.

She liked to get these girls in and out quickly, before they caused too much trouble. The fact that the girl was still vomiting made her even more determined to get it over with, she just hoped that the foetus inside the poor girl was not too formed. It was against the law and she did not want to be found out again that she was still practising. Maybe she could just pretend to remove the foetus and take her money. There could be complications and the girl could die, but she was prepared to take the chance, she needed the money for her *habit*.

"Are you ready?" She asked impatiently.

Maria nodded her head. She was too scared to speak as she braced herself as the woman held one of her legs down and told her in a stern voice not to move. But her legs were shaking so violently with her fear it was difficult to obey her. No one had told her about the pain as the woman plunged into her with the stainless steel surgical tool she was using.

"I was right, you're a good way along." The woman exclaimed as she pushed hard on Maria's stomach.

Maria lay as still as she could and endured the pain. She tried not to scream out, or choke on her vomit as she continued. The pain seemed to go on endlessly and the room began to spin, then finally she slipped into a merciful darkness.

Suddenly the woman was shaking her and there was a cold wet cloth on her forehead. The woman told her to hurry up and go, because it was against the law and she didn't want her hanging around too long in case someone reported her.

"I don't think I can go yet!" Maria cried out.

The smell of her vomit was turning her stomach again and the sight of the pan of blood on the nearby table almost made her blackout again.

Dizziness, pain and terror, tore through Maria's slight body, as the nurse shoved a piece of dirty rag between her legs, inside her knickers, to staunch the bleeding. It was almost unbearable to walk out to see the old Madame, who was waiting for her.

"Take her away and put her to bed for a few days." The nervous woman said to Madame Teresa as she held the back door open for them to leave unseen by her neighbours.

"Hurry up, no one must see you."

When the Madame saw the amount of blood on the young girl's legs, she realised that something might have gone wrong.

"Perhaps you should come and stay with me at the brothel for a couple of days until you feel better," she suggested. "I will send one of the older girls around to see your mother. She can tell her that you are helping me out and have to live in for a while."

Not that Maria's mother would care, she thought, all that her drunken mother cared about was where she would get the money for her next drink or fix.

Madame Teresa was lucky enough to find a battered old taxi, a friend of hers, driving past and he drove them back to the brothel.

Maria remembered nothing until she was put into bed in one of the bedrooms at the brothel. She could feel the wet rag between her legs and the searing pain cutting through her and she rolled over and was unconscious within a few seconds.

When the Madame came in to see Maria a couple of hours later, she found her writhing with pain and grey in the face, her lips faintly blue and she was covered in beads of sweat. She panicked and left her on the bed not knowing what to do.

***

Maria tossed and turned for two nights and two days and retained a high temperature. Madame Teresa knew that she must call a doctor or take her to one. She would call the nice doctor who visited the local charity clinic in the next town three times a week and see if something could be done. She rang the charity clinic immediately for an appointment.

When the doctor arrived he found Maria deeply unconscious and then out of instinct he pulled the grubby sheet from her body and he saw she was lying in a pool of blood that had spread around her on the bed.

Dr Martinez stared at her. Not another one, he thought as he examined her. She had lost a lot of blood and the foetus was probably still inside of her.

He did not hesitate for a moment, he picked up her thin body and ran with her in his arms to his car and placed her on the back seat and covered her with an old blanket he always kept there.

He radioed into the hospital for an ambulance and a nurse and they met him at the entrance of the brothel and lifted her gently out of his car into the ambulance.

Maria had lost an enormous amount of blood and the nurse immediately put her on a drip. The doctor tried to staunch the flow of blood, but she needed an operation to stop the bleeding and they rushed her to the hospital, with the doctor following them in his car.

Meantime Maria was in and out of consciousness on the journey.

***

When Maria eventually came too in the operating theatre she spoke to the doctor in a tearful voice.

"I must talk to you. Please." Maria said to him quietly . "Please help me. I have no one else to turn to."

"Yes, my dear of course you can talk to me. You have been through a lot of trauma." He said looking down at the young girl's pale face as she lay on the operating table.

"I need an abortion. I think I am still pregnant." She said as she grabbed him by the arm.

The words came out suddenly, hysterically; she had no idea where she was. Tears spilled out of her huge light blue eyes and ran down the hollows of her haunted face.

"Oh please, I can't have it. I can't! And I don't know what to do, where to go. I'll die of shame if anyone finds out." She was now openly sobbing with hysteria.

As the doctor washed his hands in the hand basin nearby, he thought if only I could stop all this sort of thing happening.

He walked over to her.

"My dear, I have done my best and stopped the bleeding. It will be all over soon. You may get down in a few minutes. Your baby is born and is very, very weak, I do not think she will live; we have put her in an incubator. I need to see you again in two days, time. I will come to you at the brothel; there is no need to come to the clinic again. I will give you an injection of penicillin now and some antibiotics capsules that you must take three times a day for seven days, one in the morning, midday and one at night and you must rest. Do you understand? You must rest for a few days. You have been through a lot. Leave everything to me, I will help you. You must rest though, do you understand?"

She nodded her head.

He smiled at her; she looked so fragile and so young. He felt like he could weep for her for all the pain she had been through. He had his own ideas as to who had done it, but how could he stop it happening? It was not the first time.

He had been able to staunch the bleeding but was not sure if he could save the child. He doubted also if the young woman would ever conceive again. He felt that in some ways it would be God's will, what would she do with a baby and no help? He would ask a good friend of his who was one of the founders of the clinic to help. There were plenty of women without children in the United States of America who would adopt a young baby and perhaps a teenager. A close friend of his had several connections in New York.

He looked at the burn marks on Maria's face and touched the left side of her face and examined the damage. Her skin was red and pitted where it had healed badly and he wondered how she had got burnt? He reckoned the wound could be grafted and in time would be almost invisible, she was still very young and would heal well with the right treatment and when she wore the right make-up. She was such a very pretty young girl and already had gone through so much sorrow.

Maria nodded her head as a wave of nausea rose in her throat; her head was splitting with pain, she had not eaten for three days. She clutched at the chair in front of the doctor's desk, fighting to stay upright.

"I don't want the child, do you understand me. If she lives I cannot support her, she will die anyway," she whispered through her dizziness.

Maria could hear him talking to her and the doctor's face was swimming before her eyes. She put up a hand to her face to ward it off and in doing so released her grip on the chair and collapsed onto the floor.

Dr Martinez was quick, but not quite quick enough to catch her. He knelt swiftly by her side and took her wrist in his cool fingers as he took her pulse. As Maria slowly came back to consciousness she felt the doctor's fingers on her wrist and she lay still for a moment, her eyes closed trying to gather herself together and at the same time enjoying the touch of his cool fingers on her skin.

The doctor wondered if he could in fact save the premature baby he'd handed to the matron to take to the Premature Baby Ward and have her placed in an incubator room and if she lived then get her adopted when she was strong enough! He knew someone who was waiting for a baby girl. It would certainly solve Maria's problem, she was merely a young woman herself and perhaps the baby, ***if*** she pulled through, would have a decent life yet. He would also try and find someone to adopt Maria and he thought he might know someone.

CHAPTER FOUR
FOUR MONTHS LATER

The car with two men inside turned the corner into a quieter street. The taller one glanced around at the crowded tenements at a group of children half-clothed and filthy. They were playing with their home crafted wooden toys and their shrill voices rose in the dry and foul smelling gutters.

"It can't be easy being a doctor around her," he said to his companion, Doctor Eduardo Martinez.

"That's the point; I don't turn anyone away who can't pay their fees. Working at St Joseph's Private hospital three days a week and then at St Mary's Charity hospital three days a week and sometimes even on a Sunday. Without your monetary help we could not survive. It makes me feel cleansed, after all I came from this kind of background in Mexico many years ago, but I was lucky and managed to get away. I had a mentor ten years ago when I was twenty five, similar to yourself who helped me and I often think, but for the grace of God…!" He sighed before speaking again. "I do what I can when I can."

"The girl we are going to see was to have been adopted a few weeks ago, but the couple from New York rejected her as she was too old. They have found a much younger child to adopt now, a baby girl. They gave Maria's mother some money to shut her up and I wonder how much of it she has left! Knowing her she has probably shot it into a vein or drunk it all away."

He sighed and then smiled at Antonio.

"Here we are," he leaned forward in the front car seat and pointed to a shabby, ramshackle brick and wood house through the front windscreen of the car.

***

A car door slammed and Maria went to the window, a tall figure was striding towards the front door.

Was the man actually wearing a black cape over his black suit? Was that what geniuses wore? Maria wished she could see his face, but it was concealed by a black broad-brimmed hat tilted fashionably to one side.

The car was sleek, foreign, a black Mercedes and someone was outlined through the tinted windscreen, in the passenger seat. She knew it was the doctor who had saved her.

This was going to be interesting she thought, she was about to meet her mysterious guardian angel who was going to take her away from her abject poverty.

Now she was just over twenty one years old, the man the doctor had told her about, was ready to adopt her. All the paperwork was in order at last. She was going to start a new life and leave her mother and the village behind her forever.

Maria's mother had cleaned the house a little as well as cleaning herself up a bit, for the second meeting of the night caller who was going to give her a lot of money for her daughter. She would be able to leave her hovel and go and stay with her sister and live reasonably well for the rest of her life. Her mother went to the door and greeted the tall man with her right hand outstretched and a broad false smile on her face.

"Little Maria is waiting for you in the other room. I will bring her to you." She announced as he entered the cluttered shabby kitchen.

Antonio looked at the girl's mother. He reckoned years ago she had once been a very pretty woman. She had very good bone structure, he wondered if she had come from aristocratic birth and perhaps had been thrown out by her family for shaming them by getting pregnant when she was very young. As he knew that was often the case many years ago.

Now she was a dark-haired, bone-pale face woman of around forty five or more and no longer cared about her appearance. He noticed she was above average height, but her figure had thickened out after having had four children. Even so he could tell that she had been quite a beauty in her time. Her nose was straight and her lips full and her bloodshot eyes were still an arresting pale blue colour. She stood in the shadow of the dingy room and watched him with greedy eyes as she nervously fingered a pretty pearl necklace around her neck.

"I will get my daughter," she said quietly. "She is waiting in her bedroom for you."

"Here is my little Maria," her mother announced as they came across the dingy living room.

Maria's right hand stretched out to greet him as she walked slowly towards him, watching him.

The tall stranger was standing with his back to her as she entered the kitchen and he began to turn so slowly that it seemed he emerged from the shadows of the dimly lit front room by degrees and gradually committed himself to the available light from the bare bulb on the ceiling.

He seemed to take ages for that turn to be completed, so that her arm grew tired from being extended. Her smile became fixed on her face and her whole being ached from the suspense of waiting as she stepped forward with a shy smile on her face to meet her night visitor.

Maria was aware that her mother was watching both of them intently and she wondered how much her mother had received for her, no doubt it was a great sum of money, as he was obviously rich. Yet she was not afraid of him, because she knew deep down inside that he would be a kind man and look after her. He was her future, her saviour, her wishes come true.

Antonio finally turned around and could see immediately that the girl had got her looks from her mother.

His voice was deep when he finally spoke to Maria, yet no more than a whisper.

"I'm pleased to meet you at last," he murmured softly as his fingers gently closed around her long pale hand and he took her small hand in his and his gaze slowly and deliberately raked over her face.

He was mesmerised by her as she stared back at him. He could not believe his luck. How splendid was this lovely girl, long limbed, sharp little narrow shoulders and barely formed breasts. She had pellucid skin and pale turquoise blue eyes, abundant dark hair reaching down to her waist which slipped forward over her face hiding most of her burns as she walked towards him.

She moved before him like unspooling frames of film. He knew he could make a fortune from her. He would mould her into the most fabulous model in the world. He breathed cautiously as he had a fleeting picture of this tall, gazelle-like creature, standing naked before him. She was his now, he had bought her from her greedy mother and he would make her into the most desirable woman on earth.

He was not concerned about the large burn scar on her face as he knew that it could be erased with the right plastic surgery and he knew the very people to take her to in New York and then onto Switzerland if necessary.

He could see far beyond the scar on her face, her bone structure was incredible and a kind of radiance seemed to be given off by her beauty. He wanted to photograph her just as she was.

Little Maria also could not stop staring at him and she wanted to reach out and touch his face, he was so handsome and he had such a kind face. There was an immediate bond between them and she knew she would be safe with him for the rest of her life.

His shining black, wavy hair was combed and brushed off his aquiline features and his eyes were of a shade of violet, his nose was straight, almost like a Roman nose and his lips were a perfect bow.

He wore black brogue shoes on his feet, he was tall and dressed in black designer trousers and his black shirt open to the second button and he wore a knee-length black cape around his shoulders. He reminded her of one of the heroes in the books she had read in the past.

Antonio smiled at her gently and she stopped staring at him and she too managed a smile and stood with her fingers laced together with his. She could feel the vibes through his fingers and knew he was a good man and that he would look after her and never hurt her.

"Come girl, are you ready? Have you packed your things?" He asked in a heavily accented English voice.

"Yes, I have this small suitcase, I have all that I need inside it." She answered quietly in broken English. All she wanted now was to get away from her greedy mother and the smell of the abject poverty that she lived in. She wanted to forget the past and start a new life.

Maria's mother stared at the two of them and she knew that she had made the right decision even though deep down inside of her somewhere she would miss her daughter. She realised what a bad mother she had been to Maria, but it was too late now to do much about that. The girl's future lay ahead and she would not stop that happening. She reached around her neck and slipped her pearl necklace off and placed it over her daughter's head.

"This is the only thing I have left of value now. Your grandmother gave it to me on my wedding day." Laura whispered. Her tired eyes were fall of emotional tears as she looked at her daughter probably for the last time.

Antonio watched as his protégé had no tears, no evidence of sentiment in her candid eyes as she looked at her mother and took the necklace from around her neck and put it into the small breast pocket on her little flowery dress.

"Thank you Mama," said Maria quietly in Spanish. Her eyes still lacked tears as she turned away and left the house with the man, who had paid so much for her, seemingly in her mind, for so little.

Her mother watched as her daughter walked away down the weedy footpath with the tall dark-haired man who was carrying her little suitcase and as they approached the black car that was waiting for them she waved from the kitchen window. Neither of them had turned to look back at her. She knew she would probably never see her daughter again.

The big black car moved off silently. Maria did not look back.

She had not been called Fabiana then. Antonio had agreed with her on the name she chose sometime later on when she had told him about her dreams of the future and when he started to groom her.

BOOK THREE
CHAPTER FIVE
FABIANA'S COMING OUT PARTY

Antonio realised how intelligent Fabiana was. Over the past year she had done a great deal of reading and studying. She had two private teachers, an English lady and a French tutor who taught her at Antonio's penthouse and she also did a great deal of reading and studying.

She seemed to absorb new information like a sponge, and remembered everything that her tutors and Antonio taught her. Now she spoke several languages as well as Spanish. Almost perfect English which was Antonio's mother's tongue and had also learnt Italian which had been his father's native language and her French was very passable.

Fabiana looked at the homework her private English tutor had set for her for the last time. She didn't feel like working and instead reached out for her TV control and turned it off before stretching out on the bed with her arms folded under her head.

Only two more days and she would be twenty-two years old.

There were many things she thought she might like to do. Art College perhaps in London or Paris, to study either drawing or fashion and design. She was determined one day to be not only rich, but very famous and forget her impoverished past.

At least now she had the right sort of education and it would help her for the rest of her life. Antonio had also seen to it that she would never be poor again. She knew he had already deposited a very large amount of money into a bank account for her when she turned twenty two and also given her a very large amount of shares in several of his lucrative companies that she would receive on her twenty fifth birthday as well.

She turned down the volume on the new portable TV that Antonio had given her as one of her early birthday presents and returned to the books. She must not let him down. He was not only her adopted father, but he was also her mentor and best friend and he wanted the same things in her life as he had and always had time to help her.

She was now known as Fabiana Elizabeth Donnetti. Elizabeth was his deceased mother's name and Fabiana's surname had been changed to his by Deed Poll after six months of her adoption.

She loved Antonio very much, not in a sexual way, it was deeper than that, it was more spiritual and yet she did find him very attractive, even though he was old enough to be her father.

He had taken her out of a life of poverty and was grooming her to meet the World full in the face. She always felt so proud when he introduced his protégé to his friends.

She recalled what he had said to her in the car when he had whisked her away from her mother and her abject poverty in Bogotá, Columbia.

"My little one, nobody is ever going to hurt you again whilst I am alive, I will always look after you. No one will have the power over you unless you give it to them. You are strong and have a wonderful future ahead of you."

So far, this had been true and in two days' time he was going to introduce her to his World. He had arranged her birthday party at one of the top restaurants in New York, where many famous people came to show themselves off. He had also designed a marvellous dress for her coming out, as he called it, as he wanted to show off his protégé to everyone.

Her face had healed well over the last year. No one would ever know that she had been burnt badly.

Antonio had taken her to Switzerland for the initial work on her face and then back to New York and introduced her to the best plastic surgeon in New York and now her face was beautiful once again.

Fabiana had under gone several operations over the months and now they were living in New York in his wonderful new Penthouse, which was a long way from Columbia and the sordid life that she had led. Her mother had since died. She did not even know where her sister and her brothers were.

***

Fabiana had only visited her mother twice, as agreed, when she was adopted by Antonio and then four months ago Antonio had taken her back to her village for the funeral of her mother. They were the only mourners, but at least she'd had a decent burial instead of being thrown in the Paupers' Cemetery.

Few places depressed Fabiana more than going back to where she was born. She never stayed very long on her two visits. Her mother had always been comatose lying on the couch as usual; she had not gone to stay at her sister's house after all, she had also long ago spent all the money that Antonio had given her on drugs, cigarettes and alcohol and she always begged for more when they had visited her.

The town and the old house stank of poverty, despair and failure and every time she went there, a flood of buried childhood memories came rushing back to remind her of whom she was and where she'd come from. Fabiana silently vowed to herself that she would never go back to Columbia again.

She recalled how as she had stood on the steps of the old church with Antonio's arm around her shoulders. She had looked around and she watched an old woman making her way slowly towards the old water-pump nearby and she closed her eyes to push away the image of herself as a youngster trudging up the same road towards the brothel where she had worked. As she looked around she noticed nothing seemed to have changed.

A young girl in a white bridal gown, obviously homemade by her mother, with her mother and father were approaching the church. Fabiana smiled at them and she wondered what future the young girl had. She felt a lump in her throat as she pushed back her tears.

"I understand your grief." Antonio's voice was gentle. "I still miss my parents after all these years."

He turned his face away as tears still welled up in his eyes after all this time, but he did understand her. Being there with Fabiana brought back memories with an intensity he had been unprepared for. The veil between the past and the present was so thin.

Fabiana turned to Antonio and said quietly.

"I've made a decision. I don't want my mother's old house. There are too many memories so I have decided to give it to my mother's friend who lives nearby. She has been living in a hovel for too many years she deserves it. I would also like to give her some money for looking after my mother the last few weeks of her life. Please can you help me to arrange both of these things?"

Antonio nodded his head, he understood her very well. He would ask his advocate the next day to do all the necessary paper work for her. He knew that for Fabiana another chapter of her old life was finished.

***

Until Fabiana had met Antonio her saviour, she couldn't figure out why people got so worked up about the way she looked.

For several months now she'd been staring at herself in various mirrors, trying to see what people saw when they looked at her. All she could see was that her nose was too long and so was her neck. She was very tall; she was already over six foot, practically nothing in the chest department, not to mention her long arms and legs.

If she'd been an ape she thought, they would have been very acceptable. The only thing she really liked about herself was her long, dark silky wavy hair, inherited from her father and her pale blue eyes that she'd inherited from her mother, who had once been a lovely looking woman before drink and drugs had taken her over.

She felt that her best feature, were definitely her eyes. They were very large and feline shaped in an interesting shade of pale turquoise, surrounded by her long, thick black eyelashes.

***

Fabiana threw aside her homework and ran down the long staircase to Antonio's music room where he was playing the piano. She came up to him and put her arms around his shoulders and kissed him on the side of his face. She always noticed his hands, as he played the piano because they were so long and artistic.

He turned and smiled at her, one of his secret smiles that were, only for her. Each time he spoke his hands came to life, gesturing as he did so. She suddenly wanted to feel them around her body.

She knew that he was deep in thought and probably creating something in his mind. His latest venture was interior design and he had been commissioned by a famous Italian actor to redesign his old Palazzo in Milan. She was hoping to go to Milan with him.

She also knew he had no need of the money. He accepted work only to prove to himself that he could still do it. He was always looking for new projects.

He stopped playing and looked around at his protégé. His voice was deep when he finally spoke to her.

"I know you are not interested in your homework, so just set it aside. I think you've had enough tuition now. The time has come for you to see more of the World. I want you to have tonight a good night's sleep so that you will be ready for your party tomorrow(. How about playing something on the piano for me to listen to instead, my lovely?"

She leant over him and brushed his black hair back from his forehead, with her right hand and started twirling a long strand around her fingers and laughed softly.

"Why? I am beautiful enough you said. Will going to bed early tonight make me more so?" She teased.

"Yes and because I want you to!" He said laughingly. " By the way you have not played the piano for me for some time and I want to see how you are progressing! Or am I wasting my money?" He grinned at her. It was a little game they sometime played.

"Of course I will." She grinned back at him.

She had also learned to play the piano and had a natural gift for it.

As he sat and listened to her playing, Beethoven's piano sonata no. 14, he was extremely proud of his protégé, as though she was his own child, or something of his own creating, which of course she was and would be famous in the future.

He sat and watched her. She was like an angel that had come into his life. But he knew that someday she would stretch her wings and leave him.

"Do I really have to have an early night? I am beautiful enough you said, will going to bed early *really* make me more so?" She teased as her long fingers caressed the piano keys.

"Yes it will." He smiled indulgently at her.

"There will be photographers from all over New York and also some foreign ones tomorrow. I want you to look your very best. I also have a big surprise for you, my lovely. In the meantime I would like you to have this diamond watch a little present, your real present I will give you tomorrow tonight."

CHAPTER SIX
ANTONIO'S DILEMMA

Antonio had designed a beautiful dress for Fabiana's coming out as he called it.

His top seamstress from his fashion house, Donnetti's in Milan had flown in and brought over an exquisite figure-hugging full-length silver lamé dress for her, which he had designed.

The dress clung to her lithe body and was round necked to the top of her breasts. The back was V- shaped and opened down to her waist showing off her honey coloured smooth skin. The elegant clinging sleeves were three quarters long just past her elbows.

Her Manoli silver high heel exquisite strappy shoes had been made to measure in soft buckskin and covered with crystal beads, which showed off long her slender feet.

The top hair stylist in New York had come to his penthouse and arranged her dark shiny long hair which was coiffed and pulled back off her forehead into a bunch of graded curls and tendrils; some curled down almost to her waist. A make-up artist, also from the same beauty salon had applied her make-up.

Antonio had never seen a more beautiful young woman in his life when she entered the lounge, she took his breath away and tears came to his eyes. He knew she would be his new **Donnetti** top model and take the World by surprise.

"I have something very special for you." He said quietly and handed her an ivory and mother-of-pearl jewel box.

"I would like you to wear this jewellery tonight. It was my mother's."

Fabiana opened the black velvet box and gasped, she had never seen such beautiful jewellery in her life laying inside. There was a diamond necklace with a very large diamond droplet, diamond droplet earrings to match and a diamond bracelet all set in platinum and lying on dark green velvet, twinkling in the box.

"This jewellery was given to my late mother on her twenty-first birthday especially designed for her by my father. I know that she would have wanted you to wear it tonight."

His eyes were full of tears as he took the exquisite diamond necklace and fastened it around her swanlike neck. Then he fastened the bracelet around her left wrist and handed her the earrings.

She ran to the large mirror on the wall and put on the earrings and turned to him smiling.

"Fabiana you are the most beautiful woman I have ever seen in my life. In fact for me, in the World and you will always be so." He said quietly.

***

As Fabiana entered the restaurant on Antonio's left arm, everyone was taken by surprise when they saw the beautiful honey coloured skin young woman.

Antonio felt so proud of her, as he introduced her to many of his friends and to the world of fashion and especially to the Paparazzi. He knew the party would be a great success in the World of fashion.

There were a myriad of other eager photographers waiting to take her picture as she posed and smiled at the crowd around her. Little did Fabiana know that her dream would come true and she would one day become the greatest and richest most photographed model of all time.

***

Antonio and Fabiana entered their Penthouse at 2 o'clock in the morning.

Antonio turned to her and said.

"My lovely Fabiana you were a star this evening you are now ready to become the most beautiful woman in the fashion business. I was so proud of you. I will also make you the most sort after and richest woman in the World. You will never suffer from poverty in your life again."

He took her in his arms and hugged her and she nestled into his neck. She felt so safe with him and she loved him so much in so many different ways. Then she pulled away slightly and stroked his long black hair and treasured the nearness of his body against hers.

"Antonio, I want you to make love to me tonight. I have never experienced that, I have only ever been used and abused in the past."

"You know that is out of the question. I'm old enough to be your father." He said quietly as he pulled away from her.

"But you're not, are you?" She said quietly with a smile on her lips.

He kissed her forehead and smiled back at her and then put his arms around her gently again.

"My lovely one, I think perhaps you might have had a little too much champagne tonight!"

Antonio knew that Fabiana was weaving her way into his soul. He'd never let a woman take that kind of a hold on him and he was not going to risk it with her. He pulled away from her slowly and looked down at her.

"I think we have taken this a bit too far." He said quietly.

Too far, Fabiana wondered, or not far enough! She loved him so much, deep down inside and she knew that she would never be able to be happy with any other man. Maybe he was not ready to make a commitment; perhaps later when she was a bit older his love for her would be of another kind.

Fabian's heart raced and her mind reeled, she tried to gain some sort of composure. What had she been thinking about? Maybe it was the champagne that she had drunk that evening. She should have known better than to let a kiss get out of control like that. Especially with a man like Antonio who could have any woman on the Planet and change lovers as casually as he changed his expressions.

She felt like an idiot.

"I think so too. I don't know what got into me, I'm so sorry." She replied softly.

She rested in his warm embrace for several more moments knowing that it was up to her to make the first move.

"I have an idea." She said boldly pulling him into his bedroom. "Take off your clothes."

"My clothes?"

"Yes come on." She tugged at his dinner jacket. "You'll like what I am going to do, I promise you."

Slightly embarrassed he was wondering what she was up to and obeyed her and began to undress, whilst she stripped down to her tiny white silk panties.

She watched him. His body seemed perfect for a man of his age, lean and muscular, his skin pale from non-exposure to the sun.

"You know Antonio I love your body, the way you move around when we are working together on my studies and when we play the piano together. I've wanted to touch you intimately for a long time. Come and lie down with me please."

He obeyed. He knew he had to give into her so he stripped down to his briefs and she curled up beside him on the king-sized bed. He closed his eyes enjoying the feel of her so close to his skin and relaxed. Yet he made no move toward her. He loved her so much he just wanted to simply hold her.

After a few moments she moved and knelt by his side.

"I want to make love to you, to feel you and explore you." Then she gave herself over to an examination of his body.

She ran her hands slowly over his smooth skin, barely touching his flesh, like a butterfly hovering over him, then with her mouth, kissing and stroking, probing and caressing him.

His body, even in the darkness, glowed in the light caught from the sconces on the bedroom wall and became golden.

He was more than manly to her. He was like a God, as he lay back on the white king-sized bed as she ran her hands along his body, exploring, measuring, appraising, always to her delight.

She reached into him in an intimate manner. Her lips were partially open and he could feel her small breasts brush against his chest and he felt alive with passion for her. She grazed his mouth hesitantly with her lips and then kissed him gently.

At first she was shy and then more passion was put into the kiss. She knew he wanted her and that he knew she felt the same.

Her tongue was, probing, promising passion. He pulled away from her not sure that they should be doing this. She kissed him again, her soft lips moving back and forth, round and round, increasing the pressure and her tongue slipped into his mouth tenderly.

Antonio could contain himself no longer and kissed her passionately. Theirs was a furious passion. He had ached for this moment and here she was in his arms, kissing him, holding him and he somehow knew it was right.

He slowly, worked her tiny silk panties off her lithe body.

"You know, I love you so much and I love your body." He murmured.

As she moved to take off her diamond earrings, he stopped her.

"NO, leave them on. I want you to leave them on with the rest of your jewellery."

She lay back on the white satin cushions on her great bed, wearing nothing except her shining jewels as she watched him admiring her body.

"Come, I have an idea," he said as he took her hand and helped her up and led her into the hot tub on the roof of his penthouse.

The water was warm and the magic waves seemed to caress them both as they embraced each other, their bodies melding, touching at every place, inextricably bound together.

They kissed with elegant abandon, a deep long kiss that actually made her so weak that she clung to him. As he moved his mouth from her lips to her breasts, taking in first one nipple, then the others, she felt a streak of ferocious desire shoot from her breasts to the place that his hand now reached to massage.

Fabiana drew away, looking stunned, anxious, elated even. Then taking his face in her hands, she kissed him softly, as if every taste was like nectar.

Antonio felt a shiver of anticipation as a sense of danger rippled through him.

He ran his hands down over her smooth body. Had any other woman tasted so sweet, he thought. Had any other woman tempted him beyond all reason? No, and he doubted that another ever would. He wanted to press himself against her and let her know how much he wanted her. The attraction he'd tried so hard to ignore over the years ignited into a full-blown passion for her and threatened to burn out of control.

He wanted to lay down with her for eternity and bury himself deeply within her, but as badly as he wanted to make love to Fabiana, to show her how much he loved her, he couldn't let things get to the point of no return. He had to stop.

It took all of his will power to break the sensual kiss and when he pulled away, he feared he wouldn't be able to help himself from taking her back into his arms again.

Suddenly Fabiana pulled back realising that he was also fighting a battle with himself.

"I don't know what got into me Antonio, I'm so sorrow."

She knew she'd made a complete idiot of herself, would he ever forgive her? She had teased his senses until lust had taken over his being, completely shattering any sign of reason. What kind of future could she have now, but she wanted him so much to make love to her?

He gazed at her and could contain himself no longer and kissed her back, theirs was a furious passion. He had ached for this moment and here she was in his arms, kissing him holding him and he as well knew it was wrong.

She leaned into him in an intimate manner. Her lips were closed and he could feel her small breasts brush against his chest and he felt alive with passion for her.

She grazed his mouth hesitantly with her lips and then kissed him.

At first she was shy and then more passion was put into the kiss. He wanted her and he knew that she felt the same. Her tongue was, probing, promising passion. He pulled away from her not sure that they should be doing this.

She kissed him again, her soft open lips moving back and forth, round and round, increasing the pressure and her tongue slipped into his mouth tenderly.

Then she was floating and he still stood holding her, as he felt her relax into the wonderful water, her long dark hair billowing out around her, her jewellery glistening in the warm water. He pulled her into his naked body and then he easily slipped his throbbing member into her as if they were meant to be lovers.

She gave herself entirely to him, the water and the music and their mutual cries of delight and ecstasy rose from the pool in the lush fulfilling night.

***

Fabiana lay in the shadows of his big bedroom waiting for him.

Finally he joined her and lay down beside her. She listened to his breathing and snuggled up to him.

"Hold me," he whispered. "Just hold me."

He turned to her and buried his face in the mass of her long dark hair and breathed in the scent of her. He could not explain, but he loved her too much in so many different ways. He was afraid to get hurt again, like he did after his parents died. He was afraid of losing her.

Then he let go of her and drew his right arm across his forehead and turned his face away from her and tears ran down his cheeks.

As Fabiana lay in the dark she realised that she had crossed the line and knew that the bond they had together would never be quite the same. She had teased his senses until lust had taken over his being, completely shattering any sign of reason. What would happen in the future ? How stupid of her, but she loved him so much, would he ever forgive her?

The tears ran down her cheeks as well and she quietly cried herself to sleep.

***

Over the next four nights, Antonio came to her bed, sometimes for three hours or so, more often only one hour. He did not make love to her, he just held her. On the surface he ignored her completely, except at meal times when they sat together and he just gazed thoughtfully at her across the dining table.

Finally he decided that he would leave New York for about three weeks, to go to Milan to see a client of his. He needed space to think.

Fabiana would not be on her own, his housekeeper would be in everyday to look after her and his chauffeur would take her out when needed.

CHAPTER SEVEN
ANTONIO DONNETTI'S LIFE

Antonio Donnetti was of mixed parentage. His father had been Italian and his mother English. His parents had died in a car crash when he was fourteen years old. He had been left behind with his nanny in New York when the incident had happened. His parents had left everything they owned to him and he became a child multi-millionaire overnight.

His French uncle who was also his Godfather and a very famous Barrister in Paris and his English aunt on his mother's side was his Godmother. They took him to France and became his guardians. He was too young to know at the time his father had been an arms and drug dealer and his parents death had not been an accident, it had been set up by a competitor.

His godparents sent him to The Sorbonne in Paris to finish his studies and then later to Switzerland where he studied photography.

Antonio at twenty years old received his extremely large inheritance from his late parents. He also became a magician with a camera and Worldwide famous for his unusual photography.

He could put a woman's face on the cover of any magazine in the world. When he was twenty five years old he set up the Donnetti Fashion House in Milan and then in later life he went back to New York.

As soon as he had seen Little Maria, as he called her then, he knew he could make her famous overnight when he had first met her in Bogotá, Colombia. He was living in New York at the time and introduced her to a plastic surgeon who suggested that he take her to Switzerland to a colleague of his and then he would take over from there.

Antonio knew that when she was older she would be striking. She would be a cool, tall beauty. She was like a wild gazelle.

CHAPTER EIGHT
FABIANA'S DREAMS

Ten days after Antonio had left to go to Milan, Fabiana had been having nightmares about her past and they were always the same. She felt she was trapped in one of those terrifying nightmares.

She was lying face down on the bed, on top of the sheets and the blankets. Her wrists were handcuffed behind her and a second pair secured her slim ankles. A shiny shackling chain linked the restraints, she had been violated. Marco the pimp sat in a chair, smoking a small cheroot, staring at her with a big grin on his face.

Then the nightmare changed and she was in a public square with an ornate fountain in the middle and there was a tall guitarist dressed in a red velvet suit playing his guitar.

Fabiana recalled the guitarist, it was Marco. He came closer and closer to her, drawing in the crowds.

Suddenly a young girl, no more than sixteen in a brilliant red ankle-length dress

was walking behind him, a tambourine in her hands while she tapped and shook it and she moved gracefully along the path that opened up for her. Every now and then she took a few dancing steps and twirled around.

The young girl was herself, Maria, when she was younger.

The guitarist started to strum his guitar, the tambourine rattled musically and enticingly. The girl lifted her long graceful arms above her head. A few people started to clap in time to the music. This seemed to spur her on. She began to move slowly, sensuously at first. Then faster, wheeling and dipping, stamping and flashing her long slim legs in the flounces of her crimson skirt. Her skin was smooth and dark as amber silk, her hair raven-black. Her young body slim and strong looking curved voluptuously in the dress that fitted her slim waist and hips. She was young, beautiful and exciting. The cheering crowd loved her.

Slowly the tempo of the music died down, the girl in red still dancing, the crowd now silent as they watched her in fascination.

Her tambourine had been laid down to one side and from a pocket of her skirt she took out a pair of black castanets and she fitted them to her fingers. The tempo gradually quickened. The girl stamped rhythmically. Then she stopped, and her back arched, fingers clicking the castanets rapidly above her head, she turned slowly, displaying herself, knowing her beauty, revelling in the audiences cheering and its attraction.

Suddenly she stopped dancing as she realised that the red strawberry mark on her face was in full view of her audience as her long hair fell to one side and she screamed out in terror.

Fabiana suddenly awoke and she realized that she had been dreaming again about Marco and his followers. Her face was wet with perspiration and fear.

Fabiana caught sight of herself in the mirror and screwed up her eyes to get a better look. She looked pale, with dark shadows beneath her eyes from sleepless nights that kept on plaguing her. The past she thought, has a nasty way of sneaking up on one, making one hurt all over again.

She resolved that she must to go to bed before midnight and stop drinking alcohol and taking sleeping pills every night. Alcohol only made her shake the ghosts off her shoulders and she felt so groggy in the mornings. She knew she must tell Antonio about Marco having come back into her life and trying to blackmail her regarding her past.

Antonio would understand and help her. He had been away for the last three weeks in London and Paris with his clients, but he was due back in two days' time.

***

The moment Antonio met Fabiana at the airport he realised that something was wrong. During the drive back to his apartment she was very quiet and he wondered if she was ill.

Once they were back home and he dismissed his driver, he asked her what was wrong.

"What is the matter little one? What is troubling you?"

Fabiana burst into tears and he took her in his arms and held her tightly. She told him about her nightmares and Marco.

"Oh! Antonio, what shall I do? Do you remember me telling you about Marco, the pimp at the brothel in Columbia, he contacted me two weeks after you left, I don't know how he found me. He was waiting outside of our apartment block when I went shopping several days ago, alone."

Antonio released her from his arms and they sat down on one of the large white leather sofas in the lounge.

"Tell me Fabiana. Tell me **all** about it."

"Well, I decided not to go with the chauffeur one day, about eight days after you left. It was a lovely day and I needed to walk to sort myself out.

"I have been having terrible nightmares since you were gone. Suddenly someone grabbed my hand as I was nearing Central Park? It was Marco the pimp from long ago. He insisted that we go for a coffee and he produced an envelope with several photos in it of him and me having sex as well as some of his customers, most of them were fake. He also has a photo of my child or so he says. He is trying to blackmail me. He no longer lives in Columbia. He lives somewhere here in New York. Someone had told him, most probably he beat it out of the old Madame at the brothel, and he somehow found out where we live, or where I live. He knows about you and me living together though and he wants money from me for all the photos. He has been hanging around waiting for me to go out again on my own to meet up with him, then he disappeared for several days."

She stopped for a few minutes before she continued.

"Two days ago go I went out again and he appeared as before. He has given me two days to give him five hundred thousand dollars. If I don't, he is going tell the World about me. What am I going to do? "

Fabiana burst into tears again and Antonio put his arms around her to comfort her.

Antonio knew this would happen one day. His friend Dr. Martinez who still lived in Bogotá had phoned him about one month prior and told him that the authorities were after Marco the Pimp, who had robbed a bank in Medellin and escaped to New York. The doctor had been trying to find out where the pimp was living.

Antonio had not mentioned it to Fabiana as he did not want to frighten her and he would deal with the evil man when the time came. He knew now was the time!

"My darling Fabiana, I will deal with him, but you must go and meet him and see what his terms are, he might decide he will ask for more money! You will have to stall him and tell him that it will take a few more days to get that sort of money from your bank. Then report back to me and we shall make a plan. We need those pictures. I only hope that he has not had copies made of them, could be a bluff though, I don't trust him."

***

Two days later on the steps of the big church of St. Patrick's, a tall figure stood in the dark shadows as the evening drew in. He looked like a caricature from an old black and white movie. He was furtive, dark and the type that talked out of the side of his mouth like he was always giving you some inside information. His face was partially hidden from the cold by a long black jacket with its hood pulled low over his face, as if waiting for someone. He held his head slightly to one side as if he had been in an accident or something similar.

As the church clock chimed 7pm, Antonio man hurried up the steps and into the building. His footsteps echoed on the marble floor, breaking the silence of the dimly lit building. He sat near the back, three rows from the door and pulled his cloak around him and his hat down over his face. It was bitterly cold in the great church.

A few minutes later Antonio was joined by the tall figure who been standing outside on the steps of the great church and they shook hands surreptitiously.

The dim light only partially hid the shadows of pain and sadness and the man's tall frame was bent, almost crumpled in grief and he stared straight ahead as he spoke.

Antonio felt a sweat break out on his upper lip, despite the cold. His hands were shaking and he tucked them quickly down inside his pockets.

"Don't worry; he won't get away with it." Said the other man as he stood up to go. "He will pay for it, I'll see to it for hurting her so much in the past."

Antonio watched the man go. He shivered again and dug his hands into his pockets. Playing God he thought, it wasn't right, not right at all, but what else could he do? He loved

Fabiana so much and Marco had made her life hell when she was a young teenager. The pimp must pay for his indiscretions.

The first part of the job was done, the meeting was over and now it was up to the man to carry out his orders.

Antonio stood up and walked slowly down to the front of the great church and stood facing the huge ornate gold altar. He looked up at the effigy of Christ hanging there as he made the sign of the cross, looking for inspiration. He felt the first ache of guilt and it made him strangely nervous. It was a long, long time since he'd prayed.

"Lord, please forgive me for my sins. Look after her please," he said aloud. "Look after the little one and make her safe. What else can I do Lord?"

Antonio smiled at himself praying in a Catholic Church. He had never prayed very much after the death of his parents, he had lost all faith, but here he was. Whom else could he turn to?

He shrugged his shoulders and turned to leave. He knew he should never have left Fabiana alone. The time had come to take her away from New York and introduce her to the only living family he had left, his Aunt Victoria in France and then show Fabiana to the rest of the World.

BOOK FOUR
CHAPTER NINE
PARIS AND LONDON

Fabiana looked down from the balcony of Antonio's large apartment and she could see across Paris in all its glory at night under a zillion bright lights. The Eiffel Tower in the distance lit up the sky with its thousands of coloured bulbs.

She had always wanted to come to Paris, always dreamed about it and here she was. She could hear the heartbeat of the city, the roar of the traffic, the buzz of human life and she was going to be a big part of it very soon.

Antonio had done this for her and he had promised her that they would go sightseeing over the next three days and travel down the Seine and have an evening meal on one of the bateau mouche. Visit the Notre Dame Cathedral and Montmartre. He was also going to take her shopping at Chanel and Dior.

Three days later he would introduce her to his only living relative, his aunt on his mother's side. She lived in a château in Lyon. Afterwards he was going to take her to the rest of Europe and then finally to London to meet Simon Nedler, who was a partner in the UK division of the Donnetti Fashion Empire.

***

Antonio had organized a limousine to take them to Lyon where they were dropped off at his Aunt's château.

Fabiana gazed around her in awe.

Château Elizabet, named after Antonio's late mother, had been beautifully restored.

It was originally built more than four hundred years ago and now it was an imposing massive structure of weathered Normandy stone that stood two stories high. The cupola atop the roof provided embellishment to its otherwise severe lines.

Creeper vines and rambling roses crawled over its walls of old Normandy stone and rose coloured brick, softening the whole structure. Tall chimneys punctuated the steep slope of the tiled roof and the windows were mullioned with long and narrow leaded glass panes. Fabiana knew one day it would be Antonio's.

A huge pair of entry doors constructed in Honduras mahogany swung open slowly and the tall vigilant English housekeeper, Mrs Rutledge, attired in a starched black uniform stood on the doorstep.

She wore rimless glasses and her steel grey hair was scraped back into a tight bun at the nape of her thin neck and she gave an indignant sniff as she sized Fabiana up and down.

Her face suddenly softened as she saw Antonio standing next to Fabiana.

"Good morning young master Antonio." She said quietly and then her stiff face suddenly broke into a smile."

"Good morning Mrs. Rutledge, my aunt is expecting me."

"Yes sir, we know!" She stepped to one side to allow her mistress to come forward.

Behind her walked a smart woman, a silver topped ebony cane tapping the ground with each of her strides. She was a petite woman weighing barely eight stone and she walked with shoulders perfectly squared.

Time had turned her once black hair an immaculate white. As a young bride she had worn it in a fashionable bob, but now it was styled in an updated short version that framed her exquisite face in soft waves. It was a face that had remained unlined, despite her 80 years, with the help of Botox and Collagen. Her features seemed delicate, almost fragile, until one looked into her eyes. There was a kind of power that came from their dark blue depths, the kind that came from a person of intelligence and determination. She had been a widow for over twenty years.

A tall good looking man stood at her side, he looked about fifteen years younger than she. He had been her chauffeur/butler and lover from the time shortly after her husband died.

She was of English birth, but she spoke fluent French without any accent at all having lived in France for so many years.

"Well she is very beautiful." His aunt announced, as if Fabiana did not exist whilst she looked her up and down and then turned and nodded at the man.

The tall man standing by, whose name was Ludo, acknowledged her and left the room.

The lady had a voice like cut crystal, sharp enough to slice someone to the bone, when she chose and soft enough when she liked them. She chose the first.

"My aunt Victoria," Antonio said quietly to Fabiana as he introduced her to his aunt.

Fabiana took hold of Antonio's left arm nervously.

"Antonio, outside on the terrace I think. I have family things to talk about later. " His aunt ordered. "I wish to speak to you later confidently in my study after I have shown your protégé which suite is hers during her stay."

She then turned to Fabiana and looked her up and down again.

"Come my dear," she said softening her tone somewhat. "Come with me, I will take you to your room. Dinner will be served at 7.30 pm on the terrace."

Antonio released the frightened grip of Fabiana's hand from his arm and then bent down and kissed his aunt.

He knew his aunt wanted to go back to England one of these days in the not too far future, to her large cottage in the Cotswolds and take her housekeeper and Ludo with her.

She had already drawn up her will and left him her château and vineyard along with the rest of his parent's deceased fortune.

The cottage in England and the acres of land around it would be left to her faithful staff, if they wanted it and a large sum of money. Her barrister just needed to finalise the will and for Antonio to agree to the terms.

"There you are I told you she wouldn't eat you Fabiana. It is all an act, you know. I will see you two ladies later on."

***

A week later Antonio and Fabiana arrived in Milan to be introduced to his new Italian partner and designer, Pierfabio Cuffaro. The first of many business stops for Fabiana.

BOOK FIVE
CHAPTER TEN
FABIANA IN LONDON

The temperature hit thirty degrees centigrade the summer day Fabiana and Antonio arrived in London.

They had been travelling for two and a half weeks around Europe. During this time she learnt how to show the new lines on the various catwalks, of the Dorretti ranges for the seasons and make a name for herself in various fashion magazines.

Vogue and several other top fashion magazines had already mentioned her in their write-ups:-

'Fabiana has the style and the charisma to become the most famous model in the World. She is the latest model imported from Columbia, South America. She is also mesmerically photogenic. High cheekbones, huge widely spaced turquoise eyes, slightly tilted nose and soft full mouth. Her body has the perfect combination of leanness with a small well-shaped bosom, perhaps with the aid of silicone at some time. But her long legs are her strong pulling asset, honey-coloured skin and always on display. Fabiana is six foot two in bare feet. She also has a nice persona about her and is loved by all who meet her.'

Now Antonio felt it was time to introduce Fabiana to the London side of the business.

They were staying at The Savoy Hotel in London in Antonio's suite that he kept for his visits to the UK, but on this trip he was only staying for two days. Fabiana would stay on at the Savoy until a suitable penthouse apartment was found for her in London.

Antonio would also introduce her to another of his partners, Simon Nedler who was in charge of the

London offices and then he was flying off to Switzerland on more business. He would return in about two to three months.

It was steaming hot in London that summer and there wasn't a breath of air. An angry concrete jungle caught unawares in a heatwave. But Fabiana didn't mind. Antonio told her it was the most exciting city in the world and she would conquer it as she had done with so many other cities they had visited on their trip.

The limousine from the company that Antonio always used when he visited London arrived and drove them off to Lombard Street and dropped them at the entrance of the large towering block of offices he owned.

Fabiana looked up at the white marble name above the entrance -**THE DONETTI GROUP**. It was the foremost modelling agency in England amongst other things.

She followed Antonio through the automatic chrome and glass doors into an enormous imposing foyer.

Fabiana looked around her. A thick, deep pile red carpet covered the floor. In the centre of the reception area was a big, low modern black and white marble desk. The name – ***THE DONETTI GROUP*** - was carved into a large red marble plaque on the natural stone wall. On either side of the stone wall were banks of lifts to the upper floors.

Two exquisite, well-dressed, tall, slim beautiful young women were manning the reception area.

One was a beautiful natural blonde who was on the telephone almost purring down the mouthpiece, to whoever she was talking to. The other, an equally lovely black girl was sitting in front of a computer. Their smiles and their voices were almost the same and their make-up was perfect and not a hair out of place.

The blonde had just finished talking and stepped forward to greet Fabiana and Antonio.

"Good morning Senor Antonio, it is such a pleasure to see you again. Mr. Nedler is waiting for you in his office. Please follow me."

They followed her to the bank of lifts and one of the doors opened automatically for them. Within seconds the lift reached the fourth floor and the doors silently opened and they followed the blonde along the deep dark red carpeted corridor to Simon Nedler's office.

The blonde pointed her electronic key at the door and it opened silently. Antonio and Fabiana stepped into a large office.

The blonde left quietly.

Sitting behind a large glass and chrome desk sat a man in an office surrounded by glass walls.

He rose from his desk to greet them.

Fabiana was stunned as she just stared at him. She had never seen such a good looking man in her life that oozed with so much sex appeal. Antonio had not told her much about him and that he was so good looking. All she knew about him was that he had once been a famous footballer.

Antonio watched them and saw the way they looked at each other and a strong streak of jealousy ran through him as he introduced her to Simon Nedler.

That was how she met another of the partners of Antonio's International companies.

The man behind the large desk was handsome. His pure blond looks were those of a Nordic God. His unusual pale green eyes tipped up slightly at the corners and made her think of cool water and she also noted that he sported a slight tan.

Fabian felt her heart flip and she felt a sudden rapid sexual flutter in the pit of her stomach. She could feel herself extremely attracted to him. He oozed sex appeal like no other man she'd met before and immediately knew he would be excellent in bed.

She cleared her mind, she was here as one of the partners and for a photo-shoot for one of the top fashion magazines not a date.

"Good morning. I won't keep you for a moment." Simon said quietly as he picked up his phone from the desk.

"Noreen put a stop on any calls for me. I'm very busy. I do not want to be disturbed for the rest of the day."

As he replaced the receiver he smiled one of his famous charming smiles at both Antonio and Fabiana and came round from his desk and shook hands. Lingering awhile before he let go of Fabiana's hand. Once again she felt a longing for him as she stared at him.

Simon looked at her with disbelief. In the flesh she was even more beautiful than any of the photos he'd seen of her.

She was wearing a knee length white linen two piece suit from the latest Donnetti range which showed off her honey coloured skin. To complete her outfit, a large white and black leather Donnetti handbag and black and white high heeled shoes from Manoli.

Her long, dark hair had been tied up and twisted into a knot on the top of her head, but strands of it had escaped and fell fashionably around her face, making her beauty seem even more startling for its unattended naturalness and diamond droplet earrings set in platinum glistened on her ear-lobes and her diamond Rolex watch. She wore no other jewellery.

Simon had heard that she was a legend. She was found in rags, barefooted and starving and adopted by her saviour Antonio, who had groomed her and taught her how to become a lady. She had taken the fashion World by storm.

Now here she was standing in front of him in his office in the UK and a partner in the Donnetti World of fashion. She looked so young yet he thought.

Antonio watched them and realised the strong attraction between them. He knew he had to succumb to the fact that in the future Fabiana would probably have many male admirers and lovers than most women in their lives.

His protégé had grown up and he was the cause of it. He knew she would get hurt, but she was now old enough at twenty four and a half to fight her own battles.

He also knew that Simon was not ready to have any commitment, but there was nothing he could do about that. Fabiana would find out in time.

Fabiana reckoned Simon Nedler was at least six foot three. He was lean and muscular, his blond wavy hair was fashionably cut and his face shaven. He was dressed in a black designer made to measure suit, a black shirt with the first two buttons open and hand-made black nappa leather shoes. She had heard a lot about him and his reputation in the fashion world as well as with the ladies.

Simon was a well-built, extremely good-looking man at just forty. He had made a fortune as a footballer before retiring from the game three years before. Then he had joined the fashion World and became the UK partner of the Donnetti Fashion Group.

CHAPTER ELEVEN
SIMON NEDLER

Two days after Antonio had left the UK for Italy, Simon took Fabiana to lunch.

He had introduced her to the staff and run through her part in the business. He was surprised how intelligent she was and not just a pretty face and incredible body.

He knew that they were both aware of the strong sexual attraction between them.

"Some wine?" Simon said as he held out a bottle of first-class chardonnay. I have already ordered in advance a king prawn salad with dill mayonnaise for you. "

Fabiana looked across the table at Simon and grinned at him, he was obviously a man used to giving orders to people and getting his own way.

He leaned across the table slightly and started briefing her regarding her shoot the next day with the paparazzi at the Savoy Hotel in London. He told her all the big names in the fashion world and pop world would be there to see her and what she would be wearing.

"Don't tell them anymore than they need to know about you. Do what the TV director and interviewer wants, quickly without questions, understand?"

He paused for a second or two and smiled at her.

"By the way, I have drawn something up for you to talk about. I'll send one of our drivers to pick you up at 10 o'clock tomorrow morning. You'll be at the TV studio most of the day of course. There will also be a dinner and dance in the evening. So I would suggest that you get a good night's sleep tonight."

Fabiana from across the table just sat quietly and took it all in. She realised that he was a very handsome dominant man. He would be a challenge for her. She liked challenges and strong minded men. Especially she thought when they were so good looking!

Little did he know that she already knew what to do and say! Antonio had already briefed her.

Simon took a sip of his wine before continuing.

"The garments you will be wearing tomorrow have arrived from Milan and they will be sent over to your hotel later this evening. I can also send you a hairdresser and makeup artist in the morning. If you so require. Just let me know later this afternoon."

Fabiana smiled inwardly. Antonio had left her a portfolio which she had studied but she wasn't going to tell Simon. After all she had been to many countries over the last two and half years and Antonio had taught her exactly how to play the paparazzi.

"That will not be necessary thank you. I like to do my own make-up and hair!"

***

Fabiana was resplendent in a silver and midnight blue sequinned dress with a halter neck-line that showed off her long neck and left her back bare to her waist which enhanced her honey coloured skin. Large diamond drop earrings glistened at her ears and a large diamond ring glistened on her left hand. Her long hair was swept off her face into a neat knot on her head and a few corkscrew curls were artistically hanging from the top of her head at the back.

Simon Nedler looked very handsome in his impeccable black evening clothes which set off his blond hair and good looks. They made a spectacular couple as they swayed and swirled on the crowded dance floor. Everyone else stepped aside to watch and take photos of them.

When the music stopped, they were locked somewhere between a dance and an embrace, their cheeks touching and Fabiana's heart fluttered. She usually put the shutters up when she felt more than just a physical attraction to a man. It was to do with her self-preservation. If she let men got too near too her she knew she would have to live with the pain of loss.

Simon turned her face towards him and kissed her full on the lips. Not exploratory, but hard and decisive. She felt his tongue flick into her mouth and she kissed him back. It didn't last long, but it was long enough. When they pulled back she could feel his warm breath on hers as she looked into his eyes. Both knew they were thinking of the same thing.

Several of the other dancers watched them and clapped heartily.

They both bowed to their audience.

"Let's go," he whispered and gripped her hand tightly as they left the dance floor. He beckoned to the concierge for their limousine to come and pick them up.

***

Simon's apartment was only two blocks away and they didn't speak until they got to the front door. Fabiana was lost for words, but she could feel her heart beating violently. She wanted to stop now, but she couldn't. She knew what was going to happen, but she couldn't think beyond that.

"You OK?" He whispered as he punched out the code to open the great entrance door to the apartment block where he lived and they hurried inside towards the elevator to go up to his Penthouse.

Once inside he turned to her and pulled her towards him. He was breathing fast as he ran his hands softly over her face and neck and she could feel his hard manhood pushing against her. He touched her breasts and she put her arms around him and kissed him passionately.

Fabiana nodded her head.

He pulled away and started tugging at her dress.

Jesus! She wondered if they were going to make it to the Penthouse, but she didn't want him to stop. She was breathless. What was the matter with her? She'd never felt quite like this before.

The private elevator came to a halt and the doors opened silently into the front room of the apartment.

"Come on, let's go in." He said as he took her hand and pulled her inside and quickly pressed the button to close the door.

They fell against the wall. She kicked off her Jimmy Choo shoes and shrugged off her short sequinned jacket. He was on his knees in the hallway, pulling at her dress until it was down around her ankles and she kicked it to one side, while he was easing her navy blue lace thong down her soft thighs until they were around her ankles too and she kicked them away as well.

She could see the living room bathed in subdued lighting and very soft music being piped through the apartment as she looked around her.

He lifted her up and took her into his bedroom and placed her gently onto the circular king-sized bed and looked down at her.

"You are a very beautiful young woman. I am going to make you realise that and to enjoy it before the night is over." He said softly.

Again he began to caress her slowly; his eyes open to watch her reactions. It had been many years since he had felt like this about any woman, but he did not want her to see the chink in his armour. He didn't really want to throw himself into a full blown love affair again after the last disaster, but he couldn't stop himself.

He ran his fingers across her stomach, his index finger made a small circular movement on her skin that sent her mind swirling and then slipped his tongue into her navel and upward over her pert breasts until she felt his breath, scented by her own body, against her lips. It tasted wonderful and so erotic and she whimpered with pleasure.

"You are mine," he whispered. His hand slowly lowered and Fabiana fought the compulsion to reach his hand and hold it in place as she felt her body tingling with passion.

Gently he breathed into her ears and her mouth. His lips sucked at her eyelids, her cheeks, her chin and her lips. His tongue tickled her soft throat and then slowly he made his way down to her pert breasts again and gently nibbled at each nipple in turn. His hands squeezed her little pink nipples and he pulled her towards him and then released her. Inch by inch, his hands and mouth discovered her body, leaving no secret place unfound.

He slowly led her into a new and thrilling, but frightening world. He knew he was all-powerful as his fingers travelled delicately over her body again, touching, probing, and sliding into every part of her body, until his hand moved towards the division of her thighs. At the bottom of her triangle of curly soft dark pubic hair his index finger found her little sex bud, no bigger than a pea and he started to gently and rhythmically rub it until it became engorged and hard.

Slowly she relaxed, her body surrendering to the pleasure of his touch.

The scent of his aftershave was tingling her senses and made her want to bury her nose in his thick blond hair. She did not know that any man could be so sex. Her body seemed to melt and she was no longer in control, it lifted her beyond anything she had ever felt. She felt light headed and yet as taut as a bow beneath his fingers and she could hardly breathe with the ecstasy of his touch. She could feel her nipples hardening against his warm skin.

Panting and bewildered, she opened her eyes and above her in the candlelight she saw his smiling, triumphant face.

"Open your legs," he ordered suddenly.

She stiffened at the command, so totally contrary to the way he had just made love to her but his tone demanded her submission. She knew she must surrender to him.

Quivering she moved her legs slightly apart. She felt timid and guilty, her heart pounded against her ribs with anxiety and she felt unbearably vulnerable as she parted her legs further part.

Little did she know that he had another side to him?

She watched him through half opened eyes and noticed that his interest seemed curiously objective and she watched his eyes narrow as he looked down at her as if he were a connoisseur examining a hothouse flower surrounded by pink petals and nestling in a soft dark nest of hair.

He stared down at her face.

" Exquisite," he murmured and his hands lingered around her waist as he looked at her and then he pushed her legs further apart and continued his clinical exploration of her love tunnel and pulled her sex lips apart and lowered his head and licked her love bud, until once again her body ignored her mind and the excitement she felt from his probing took her to the upper realms of ecstasy that triumphed over her shame at being so rudely scrutinised.

She screamed out with pleasure and closed her eyes as he buried his head between her legs. Fabiana shrank away, squirming slightly beneath his touch. Her brain tried to pretend that it didn't know what was happening to her body as she climaxed again and again.

Simon raised his head and looked up at her as he slipped his hand between her thighs.

"Now admit to me that is what you want." He whispered harshly.

"Perhaps it isn't." She said also in a whisper. She felt drawn to him as she had never been to any man. This was different, especially when he kissed her.

Little did she know that this would be common practice with him!

He didn't dare ask her what she meant, but only looked at her and her eyes were beckoning him with an openness and love for him that was so evident; he could not mistake their invitation. He knew the time had come not to lose his heart again to any woman. He was so afraid that he would with her.

In the morning when they awoke they lay facing each other, their bodies pressed close. Simon kissed her throat and her face and ran his hands over the smooth curve of her back. He wanted her so much, it hurt. He touched her lips with his fingers.

"Hold me." He whispered.

She pushed her hands to the side of his head and held him closely to her and slowly felt the tension in his body dissolve.

He knew he could fall in love with her so easily but also that it was not the right time in his life. He also knew they would both be hurt but he had so much to do before he settled down with her.

***

Over the next five days Simon showed Fabiana around London and introduced her to many influential people.

They made love again at his apartment and she stayed overnight twice.

He also found a Penthouse to rent for Fabiana not far from where he lived and two days later Fabiana moved into her fully furnished penthouse.

They dined that evening out at one of the top restaurants in London and she suggested they go back to her place for a change. She wanted to see how he would react in her domain.

***

They did not make love that night, both of them seemed ill at ease.

"Hold me, tightly," Simon whispered. "Just hold me. He buried his face in the mass of her fine long hair and breathed in the warm scent of her. He could not explain to her, but he loved her too much and he was afraid to get hurt again.

Several hours later he awoke. He looked down at her beside him in the first light and could see the tawny glow of her skin, the tiny hairs on her arms and neck. He kissed her lips and she woke instantly.

"I have to go Fabiana, before it gets too light. I have a very busy day in front of me. Take care of yourself." He said quietly.

He held her for a moment and then turned away from her gently and stood up, pulling on his shirt. He felt as if his heart had broken.

"I'll see you later in the office. Don't be late. I have some important news to discuss with you."

Simon took her in his arms and kissed her long and hard before leaving.

She heard the whine of the lift and turned over in her bed and gazed up at the ceiling. She suddenly had a premonition and wondered if she would ever see him again after his talk to her in the bedroom. She wondered what he had in mind. He had been very quiet the night before and not wanted to make love to her, just to hold her in his arms.

***

When she arrived at the Donnetti office to join Simon for lunch, he casually told her he was going away for several weeks or even months on business to Thailand to promote the new Donnetti range which Antonio had organised. She was now to run the business in the UK.

He told her Antonio had left a message on his mobile phone and told him to drop everything. There was a first class ticket waiting for him at Heathrow for the afternoon flight to Thailand and he had to pack immediately.

Antonio had also told him that Fabiana was more than capable of running the business whilst he was away and he would keep in touch with her and she could move into his office.

***

Fabiana hated being hurt, she loathed the humiliation. She hadn't heard from Simon for lost over three weeks, which was too long even for him. No matter how much she loved him, he would have to change. The one thing she had learnt from the past was that no man ever changed his ways!

Maybe she was not meant to find a man; perhaps this was how the rest of her life was going to be.

Simon had still not contacted her.

Maybe she should forget him, indeed forget all men. She did not need him, he needed her and she was at the top of her career. Besides she was also a partner in the Donnetti business and Antonio was always there for her.

In the course of her career she had worked with plenty of extremely good looking male models, actors, footballers and rock stars. Their seductive faces and sexy bodies graced the bedroom walls of millions of women all over the world. But no man had come even close to the kind of impact that Simon had on her and not just her, she had learnt, but to other women in the past.

Since Simon had left her she had seen him on TV and in the newspapers, with glamorous women on his arm and all the female interviewers always seemed hypnotised by his spectacular, long legged frame and seduced by his sexy voice. He'd obviously forgotten about her. She wondered if he would ever return.

Antonio never mentioned Simon during their long phone calls nor did she. He just told her she was now completely in charge of the London based businesses and also some in Paris when required.

***

One cold evening in November she decided to take a walk along The London Embankment. She needed to think about her future. She was still unsure of herself sometimes in so many ways, but no one ever saw that side of her anymore. She knew she didn't have to act out a role to please Antonio as she often did to everyone else in the World.

She was running things well at The Donnetti offices and Antonio praised her over the phone. Again he never mentioned Simon to her.

The cold brought tears to her eyes. She wrapped her luxurious full length Ranch mink coat more tightly around her slim body and pulled the fur hood down more over her face and walked for at least an hour and a half along the Embankment. She hoped no one would recognise her even though she wore heavily tinted sun-glasses.

When she returned to her penthouse she decided that she would forget Simon as Antonio had suggested and push him out of her thoughts. It was time for her to move on to another era. She was now thirty five years old, even though she looked younger and about time she found herself a suitable husband and perhaps have children and settle down to a normal life.

The walk had made her mind clearer and she decided that she would have a glass of white wine, a nice Chardonnay perhaps, a hot bubble bath, shave her legs, remove her nail polish varnish, pluck her eyebrows and wash her hair. Something she rarely did on her own these days, as she usually went to a beauty parlour in the West End or her favourite beautician came to her apartment.

She dried herself, perfumed herself and then changed into her new La Perla white satin pyjamas and took ages painting her long finger nails. Next time she went to the beauty parlour she thought perhaps she would have her nails gelled perhaps, they looked so much better.

She stood studying herself in the large wall to ceiling mirror as if the image staring back at her could tell her the reason for Simon breaking off their affair. It did not. She still thought about him, but he was fading from her mind. She also noticed she had lost a lot of weight.

Fabiana liked what she saw and thought it made her look more mature. She no longer had problems about her looks. Thanks to Antonio, she was very confident about herself now. She was a tall young woman with a face more striking than beautiful, but the camera loved her and so did her dedicated followers. Her hair was her best feature, dark almost black, thick and naturally wavy falling almost to her slim waist. She knew she looked good on the catwalk, but these days she did less and groomed the young models of her choice for shows. She would always make a courtesy appearance though at the beginning and the end.

Wherever she went of course, out to dinner or similar, she would wear her own creations designed by herself and she travelled more and more over Europe at shows.

Her pale turquoise eyes were large, sharp and intelligent. With her delicate bone structure she had a fine face which she was well aware attracted some men, but frightened others away, but that was all right, she would not have been interested in wimps anyway or handsome men that found her challenging their good looks.

Human nature is a curious thing she thought, everything happens for a reason!

BOOK SIX
CHAPTER TWELVE
SIX MONTHS LATER

It was a wonderful balmy evening in early June.

Her black company Mercedes limousine pulled up slowly and came to a halt in a long line of similar cars outside of The Hyde Park Hotel in London, where the dinner after a private fashion show for future buyers, that had been held earlier in one of the enormous conference rooms of the Donnetti building, was to take place.

Fabiana emerged gracefully from the large company vehicle as her handsome bodyguard who was sitting up front with the driver stepped from the rented limousine, opened the rear door and she smiled broadly at the people around her as she was ushered forward by him. They were almost blinded by the photographers as their equipment flashed while they took photos from different angles. She stopped and smiled and paused for several moments, to say a few words to some of the paparazzi. She knew how to play them, they adored her.

She was attired in a long white satin evening gown, designed by Donnetti Fashions, from her new range - **THE FAB RANGE** - which she was promoting that evening.

The lovely dress draped elegantly from her left shoulder and was slit up midway to her honey coloured right thigh. Her long dark hair was swept up and caught into a French pleat held one side of her head with silver clips and the rest of her dark wavy hair falling down from the pleat that showed off her graceful neck and her left shoulder to perfection.

She also wore a pair of the new - **FAB RANGE** - high-heeled strappy silver beaded shoes and held a small clutch handbag to match.

Fabiana was now under the spotlight, dressed all in white and silver, a gleaming silver taper of tanned skin and flowing hair. Her long tanned legs moving gracefully as she walked slowly to the entrance of the hotel.

Her handsome bodyguard led her forward again into the hotel foyer.

***

It was now just over a year since Simon had broken up their affair. He had at last phoned her from Thailand and told her he was no longer in love with her and could not work with her. He also told her, he did not want to settle down at this point in his life. He was staying in the Far East and starting up his own business in Thailand.

He had sold the majority of his Donnetti shares in the company to Tristan Eves the famous Rock and Movie star who was shortly retiring from the music world and Mr. Eves would be contacting her shortly for a meeting.

She had been completely broken hearted at the time, but she knew she must not let her heart rule her head. She would finally be meeting Tristan Eves for the first time that evening and she intended to enjoy herself at the party and maybe she would meet someone else in the near future.

Antonio was in Milan at the time and she had not seen or heard from him for several weeks either. She was very upset that he was not there by her side for the launching of her new range of clothes, shoes and accessories.

***

As Fabiana walked through the great hotel doors and into to the elegant banquet room, the hum of conversation floated toward her. Her bodyguard was discreetly shown to a small table nearby by one of the waiters.

She glanced around and nodded and smiled to several people that she knew by sight. The maître di' of the restaurant came forward and showed Fabiana to her table. There were two places set at a large round table and already there was someone seated at it.

A tall handsome man, in a made to measure black evening suit, rose from his chair as the maître di' pulled out her chair. She sat down and then the man introduced himself before he settled himself down again.

"Good evening Fabiana I believe we shall be partners soon."

His voice was deep with a slight American accent when he spoke to her. He held out his right hand and smiled at her.

"Tristan, Tristan Eves, pleased to meet you at last."

She looked across the table at him.

So this was the famous Tristan Eves she'd heard about from Antonio, but had not met until now! Apparently he was of English descent, but spent most of his time in America.

He was a legend in the music industry. He also owned one of the biggest media companies in the World and he was equally known for his amazing ear for new talent.

She was taken back slightly he was the most magnificent man she had ever met. She had heard of him, but she had to admit to herself that she had been taken completely and utterly by surprise seeing him in the flesh.

So **he** was going to be the new silent partner whom Antonio had chosen in her Company!

She thought he was more handsome in real life than he was in press photos. His eyes were blue, like aquamarine, they seemed so beautiful and they reminded her of cool sea water.

His hair was black as a raven's wing and combed back off his perfect aquiline face and curled slightly at the base of his neck. His face was handsome, a sensual mouth and intelligent blue eyes that crinkled in fine lines when he smiled. Up close she saw that his eyes were actually a mixture of dark blue and turquoise. Quite similar to her own she thought.

For a fleeting moment she thought if they were married and had children they would have the same eyes. Then she reprimanded herself for being so stupid.

His eyes were his best feature. Wide set and very long black eyelashes and she blushed when he stared at her. He also sported a California tan.

Here she was sitting next to him and looking at this gorgeous rock and movie star that she was feeling faint at the sight of him. She had never quite felt like that about any other man since her breakup of Simon.

Fabiana judged him to be about forty five years old. She couldn't keep her eyes off him. She also noticed that he was wearing a cream silk shirt, opened to the second button, from Gieves and Hawkes of London and at the cuffs of his shirt were platinum cufflinks with his initials in gold.

Tristan also was scrutinising her and he had wanted to meet her earlier when the deal had been done, but she had been away on a photo-shoot in France. She looked very interesting as well as very beautiful and he noticed the slant of her delicate cheekbones.

He casually filled her glass with the champagne that was on their table as he was speaking to her, so he had a minute or two to sum her up as he listened to her soft voice with her, *too* perfect English, masking a slight lisp of accent.

He liked what he saw and knew she would be just right for him as a wife and he could keep his secret. She would also take the onus off him and knew if he married her he could keep up his charade of being a famous sex symbol in his new World of famous cosmetics and fashion industry. He was also thinking of expanding and introducing male fragrances with his signature on them.

"You work for Donnetti?" He asked casually as if he didn't know that she owned part of it.

He met her brooding candescent stare for a moment and smiled at her.

"I **am** Donnetti. I own three quarters of it now. I understand that you have bought Simon Nedler out and you are now the mysterious silent partner who has joined us!

***

Two days later Tristan caught sight of Fabiana in Harrods, shopping without her usual entourage.

Catching sight of her he wound his way towards her and stopped her and asked for her advice on some jewellery that he said he was buying for a friend to take back to California in a couple of months' time.

Fabiana had been thinking about him and was still slightly bowled over by him and realised she wasn't the only one who'd noticed, but she advised him about some jewellery and as she smiled at him he thought she looked even more beautiful than the first time he'd met her.

Men as well as women turned to follow their progress as they walked through the great store. Many female and male eyes around them flickered with admiration and envy.

Tristan thanked her for helping him and invited her to lunch with him.

She politely refused as she made a little dismissive gesture because she wanted to see what his reaction would be!

"I never lunch with strange men as a rule; however if I do, I ask them first." She smiled mischievously and turned to walk away slowly.

He followed her and took her by the arm.

"So are you going to invite me then?" He grinned.

"I think you have passed the test." She laughed. "So, where are we going then?"

"I know just the place in Virginia Water, just outside of London if you would like a nice drive in my new car! Also we should have some privacy there." He suggested.

His car, a brand new red Bentley Continental, was parked behind Harrods in their special parking area for certain customers and one of the young valets who was a fan of Tristan's and in great awe of him, brought it around to the front of the large store and handed it over to his idol and they drove off.

Neither Tristan or Fabiana spoke very much to each other during the journey, but suddenly he broke the silence.

"We'll be there shortly I think you will like the restaurant, it is an old converted country pub by the river, that's recently been refurbished. I've wanted to see it for some time. I used to go there a long time ago before it had a facelift. When I was a student over here actually! Also we shouldn't be too disturbed by any of my fans and yours of course!"

The voice, the beguiling accent, the closeness of him so unexpectedly, took her breath away completely. She looked up with a dazzling smile and his aquamarine gleam of eyes quickened her heart absurdly.

Despite herself she was struck how handsome he looked. His tailored navy blue suit hugged his muscular frame like a glove. His hair shone black as he ducked to clear one of the low beams in the restaurant as they entered and a waiter came forward and led them to a table for two near the window overlooking the well-kept gardens.

It was a long luncheon. Tristan noticed that she ate very little, using a fork most of the time as she pushed the food around her on her plate. She turned her wineglass by the stem several times, but did not raise it to her lips as he studied her carefully.

She was dressed quite casually in a white silk shirt tucked into her blue designer jeans and navy blue medium heeled suede ankle boots. Her long black hair was pulled back off her face into a thick ponytail. She wore a single strand of pearls around her neck. He vaguely wondered who had given them to her.

He also noticed that for a woman who made a fortune wearing make-up and perfumes she seemed to wear very little. The skin on her face was flawless.

He had heard that she was a legend. She was found in rags in Columbia, barefoot and starving and sold to her saviour, Antonio, who groomed her and she ended up in Paris and then came over to England and became an icon. Every woman of her age group wanted to look and be like her.

***

They often dated but Tristan never wanted to have sex, he said he was old-fashioned and they should wait until they were married.

Four months later after their first meeting Fabiana and Tristan were quietly married in a small church in the New Forest, in Hampshire in the UK. Only one local photographer and one of the Press were invited.

Antonio came back from a long trip in South America and gave her away and left shortly after the small reception to return to London for a month to train a new manager for the Donnetti Corporation before he left for New York.

Shortly afterwards Fabiana and Tristan moved to California, U.S.A.

BOOK SEVEN
CHAPTER THIRTEEN
FABIANA'S SHOCK

Fabiana had not realised at first that Tristan was gay until he told her six months after they were married, but he didn't want a divorce as he had to keep his sexuality a secret. This was the reason that they had not had penetration from the beginning. He had always made some sort of excuse when she mentioned it and both of them were always very busy with their businesses and often away from each other.

He also told her that they had to keep up the pretence for the sake of both of them and to keep up the illusion for his fans worldwide. It could also damage the Donnetti Company if it got out and was made public.

***

Tristan sat across the dining room table one evening at their home in California when he told her his secret.

"I'm offering you my complete attention darling, with no sex." Tristan said quietly as he pushed his food around on his plate.

Fabiana looked at him in horror, now she knew why he was always making excuses not to make love to her and spent a lot of time without him.

"I don't mind if you have a lover Fabiana, but one thing I will say to you is, if you do have an affair, please be discreet, if we are found out, it will be the end of both of our careers. The only other persons who knows about me, are my Agent and Antonio as far as I know. It has been a well-kept secret and if it gets out we shall all be ruined. I know you want a child, so I am quite happy to supply my semen for you!"

Fabiana's eyes looked huge in her face and she forced herself to keep breathing and not faint as he told her. Every breath which she took demanded a conscious act and a specific instruction to her brain to stop shaking as she listened to what he was telling her.

Now it all made sense that he kept on telling her he would be away a lot, or he was too tired when he returned to make love to her.

She'd been horrified when he told her and she knew then that having a child by him was not impossible, but she was not prepared to do so. Once again she felt that life had punched her in the face.

Tristan had made the suggestion, that they could use his sperm or perhaps someone else's. It could be arranged quietly and his fans would not know anything about it. She firmly refused, she would divorce him when the time was ready.

She decided not to run to Antonio immediately, she would try and sort it out herself and tell him when she was ready.

Antonio left the everyday running of the UK Donnetti office to her anyway. He had left shortly after their wedding and he rarely kept in contact with her. She wondered if he was jealous, he seemed very angry whenever she did manage to speak to him on the phone he was so abrupt with her. He was not his usual self.

***

A year had passed since Fabiana's life had been shattered and she and Tristan still did not know how to react to each other when they were together and to lead a double life when no one else was around them. To the World outside of their life they were still seen as the perfect couple.

Every night they would lie in the king-sized bed with their backs turned. They were terrified that they might touch each other involuntary. She had spoken to him about separate bedrooms, but he didn't want his fans to know and he certainly didn't trust the housekeeper to keep her mouth shut and let it out that they had separate bedrooms.

He did not spend much time with her anyway, so she spent a lot of time on the cat-walks in various countries and running her company.

Fabiana knew his guilt was heavy and now separated them. They would have to continue to work it out. Thank goodness they did not have children she thought. Perhaps they could remain friends and be civil about a divorce. That would be the best solution and she did like him and they did look good together.

She had promised Tristan to keep it a secret under her terms for the time being and she remembered saying to him.

"Do you think I honestly want your sperm after all this. I will make a pact with you to save my face and your reputation. I will stay with you until such time when **I** want a divorce. It could be two years or even five years, I don't know yet. If you stray from our pact I will tell the World and you will be finished. Just make sure that you make it discreet."

She stared at him coldly before continuing.

"You can stay here in California and work if you want to, but I will return to England for a certain amount of time and tell everyone in the company that I am now running the London side of the Donnetti business completely. You can concentrate on your music or whatever. We shall meet up occasionally just to keep up the impression that we are still a happily married couple. **Understand**?" She shouted at him with rage.

Tristan just nodded his head. He knew she meant it. He realised how much he was hurting her and yet in his own way he really did love her. He hoped there was a chance that at least they could remain good friends in the future.

***

After six months Fabiana finally told Antonio about her fake marriage and he agreed with what she had told him. Once more she had run into his arms for help. She was unaware that he already knew about her husband.

***

Fabiana felt very frustrated, she'd not had any sex for nearly over a year since she'd arrived back in England.

She decided to have a shower. When she had dried herself she lay back naked on her big bed in her penthouse in London and started to slowly caress her body. She cupped her breasts in her hands, then she released them and ran her hands slowly over her naked body and down towards her pudenda. She opened her legs gradually and slowly let the fingers of her right hand find the outer and inner folds of her labia and then her clitoris below her pubic bone and softly caressed it. With her left hand she held her vibrator firmly and pushed it between her legs. She could feel the vibrator whirring and she teased her clitoris until she could slowly feel herself coming to a wonderful climax.

Recently she often brought herself to a climax manually, but she needed the real thing, she felt it was time to find herself a 'fuck buddy', as some men were called. One she could trust. She'd overheard two of her new models at a show talking about their sex life and listened carefully to what they said.

At the time Fabiana thought it was amusing, but not anymore.

BOOK EIGHT
CHAPTER FOURTEEN
TRISTAN EIGHTEEN MONTHS LATER

Tristan's cock shuddered and jerked in the young man's hand, his testicles aching for release. He could feel the young man's smooth skin pressing against his back as he rubbed himself back and forth over his body. His curly blond pubic hair pushing against his taut buttocks as the young man ran his hands over his fit body. His hips gliding back and forth over his muscular backside.

Tristan liked it when the young man took control as he was the one who usually did this when he was with one of his young male lovers.

"Turn around," said the young man quietly.

Tristan slowly turned around and faced him. His eyes were slightly closed and he opened his mouth as he felt the young man lean into his fit body and his full lips crushed his tongue into his mouth moving over his tongue, as he responded avidly. He felt his hands encircle his waist, pulling him towards his erect organ that stood out proudly.

The tall young man was just the right height for him. His hands slid down over the young man's buttocks and cupped them tightly as he squeezed them cruelly in his powerful grip. His own penis pushed hard against him, holding him firmly against his muscular body, then he savagely turned him around and lifted him onto his rigid penis thrusting into him with savage movements and they fell onto the huge bed as he spread his long legs open beneath him.

Tristan liked to be the dominant one, but this young man did also and he knew they would have a savage affair for some time. He was fed up with the one night stands that he used to enjoy and he was afraid of catching some disease from them. He'd read somewhere that Aids was becoming rife in certain parts of the World. He knew his secret was not known to his fans and that was the main reason he was still married to Fabiana to prove to the World that he was straight.

Sometimes he wondered how long he would be able to keep up the façade. His relationship with Fabiana had been an up and down time over the last two years for them both, with Fabiana's sudden move to England and his staying in the States and travelling to the UK to see her occasionally.

Lately in the Press there had been talk of their marriage hitting a rocky patch and more recently the rumours of Tristan's fling with an up and coming American male star.

Despite earlier denials, it seemed that the couple were about to show the World how much in love they still were by shortly renewing their wedding vows at a small church in Hampshire, in England?

To make the day special they'd planned to invite one hundred guests along with the Paparazzi on their third wedding anniversary to try and kill the rumours.

***

Tristan recalled their meeting with the Paparazzi a couple of months before when she was visiting him in America .

Fabiana had looked her usual beautiful self and Antonio had contacted her and told her to call a press conference to try and kill the rumours that were going around about them.

Tristan looked at her that evening in her black tailored linen trouser suit as she spoke:-

"We're a couple, but we are also independent. Tristan is my priority, but when he's away on tour I take the opportunity to focus on my own career of course. I work because I want to. I enjoy it and Tristan likes me doing it. He wants me to be busy and active. You know I'm not convinced he would want someone who was a full-time housewife. Not that there's anything wrong with that, but that's not the person he fell in love with originally. We have no plans to have children yet. It would not be fair on them always leaving them with a nanny."

A source also said that *Trist* and *Fab* were thinking about renewing their vows. It was something they'd wanted to do for a while, to show everyone how much in love they still were. The source also said they'd had a tough time with all the reports that their marriage was suffering since Tristian had come back from his long tour.

Fabiana smiled at the audience around her and stepped aside as a photographer flashed her picture, then another and another as her famous husband took his place beside her and held her hand as he too smiled for the cameras.

***

Fabiana sat at the breakfast table in Antonio's apartment that she often used when she was in Paris, especially when he was away and on the front page of one of the top newspapers in Paris, Le Figaro, there was a picture of her husband with a young man at a night club in California kissing each other in one of the most famous Gay Bars. He was seen leaving the Gay club four in the morning.

She read the article slowly; Tristan had obviously broken their pact.

'Tristan Eves the famous rock star has had a secret affair with an exotic young man in Hollywood for several months. He was seen in a nightclub in Los Angeles with Adam Sinclair, Hollywood's hottest new male film star and singing sensation. It would appear that Fabiana's husband was seeking solace in his arms in an hotel after their night out after feeling abandoned by his famous model wife, who was away again in Paris, France for yet another shoot for Vogue Magazine.'

The article went on to say:-

'Tristan had sent several graphic texts messages to the young star over the last few months. He had swept him off to his suite at the Beverly Hills hotel, to the astonishment of his bodyguard and driver for a night of passion. Since this has been revealed there is now a string of young men saying they have slept with him as well in the past few years.

Tristan Eves has been touring the States for over six months and during this time his wife was only with him for a couple of weeks. Obviously Adam is giving him what he is lacking from his famous wife.

The warning signs were there, but it is said by his Press Agent that she ignored them. She was not available for comment.

A certain, close male friend of the couple said that Tristan felt badly let down and would never have cheated on his wife if she had stayed with him for the rest of his tour, instead of her furthering her career. He also said that she was a selfish bitch who did not care about her husband.

A guest at the hotel overheard them arguing over the phone. Tristan was shouting at Fabiana on his mobile as he walked along the corridor to reception.

***

Fabiana turned on the large TV on the wall and behind the newscaster, on the screen, was the face of the young man who was at the centre of the Tristan affair.

Adam had broken the silence the night before to reveal to the TV reporter his relationship with the famous Rock Star. Adam said he was his friend and lover to the lonely star as his marriage to the great Fabiana was under intense strain and that his wife was just a selfish, rich bitch that did not care about her husband, that was why he'd become a homosexual.

Fabiana smiled bitterly at the picture of her husband and the young man. Little did the press know her husband was actually bi-sexual and how he really behaved behind closed doors! The young man went on to say that Tristan had wanted a family and she had denied him one because of her career. Tristan also alleged that his wife and he had not slept together for over several months.

The young man also claimed that his affair with Tristan would never have got off the ground if Fabiana had been with her husband in America to see to his needs.

Fabiana recalled talking to the paparazzi two years before:-

'We're a couple, but we are also independent. Tristan is my priority, but when he's away on tour I take the opportunity to focus on my own career. I work because I want to. I enjoy it, Tristan likes me doing it or so he said in the past. He wants to be busy and active. Actually I'm not convinced he would want someone who was a full-time housewife. Not that there is anything wrong with that, but that's not the person he fell in love with.'

She recalled the number of times in the past how Tristan had shouted at her, struck her and been drunk or high on drugs. He had also forced her to give him anal sex with a dildo and he had pretended that he was a woman.

She'd found out over the years he was a manipulative, scheming control freak. If she had known at the beginning, she would never have become involved with him, let alone marry him.

He'd shouted at her once under the influence of drugs and alcohol and told her he'd only married her to keep his image going. She had taken the blame to save her reputation. But one day she would tell the World when the time was right.

She'd never let the World know over the last few years of her marriage how unhappy she was, not even Antonio until fairly recently. He of course had come to her aid.

She wondered if he had in fact, set Tristan up with the young man.

Antonio had been right and foreseen what would happen, and she had alienated him by telling him, he was too jealous and possessive of her. He had walked out of her life for a long time the day after she had married Tristan. She had been so naïve then. Once again she felt so hurt and deluded with her life

Fabiana recalled the conversation she'd had with Antonio.

"Antonio, I am no longer the naïve girl that I was when you first met me. I have grown up and come to love you very much over the last twenty four years. I am now a renowned model and business woman thanks to you. We have a bond between us that no one can ever break. I want a child and my husband cannot provide me with my desire. He is gay, and before he comes out of the closet and the whole World knows it. I must conceive. I have to keep face. This is the last favour I will ever ask of you. Please help me Antonio."

She knew now was the right time for a divorce, hopefully it could be done amicably. She would return to England and quietly divorce Tristan. She knew now his career could be finished. Antonio no longer wanted him as a partner in the Donnetti group either. He would pay him off handsomely for her sake.

***

It was a wonderful evening in early June in London.

Fabiana emerged gracefully from the large white stretch limousine as her new bodyguard Marc Linford, as well as being the driver of her white convertible Jaguar on occasions, opened the rear door.

Marc had fallen under her spell the first time he had met her when she interviewed him in her office at the Donnetti building three months previously.

He wore a black designer suit with a dark grey shirt with the top button open, black leather Patrick Cox shoes and stood alongside of her watching her every movement.

Marc was a tall, handsome, young man with dark blue eyes and hair the colour of fresh straw, trimmed close at the side with a sweeping wave over the top. He had a sharp strong-looking jaw line with a slight cleft chin and high cheekbones. His firm mouth was curled slightly in the right corner, a mocking laugh in his eyes as he watched her. He was trim, movie star sleek with a perfect fake tan and the caramel tint emphasised his aqua blue eyes. He was very much in love with Fabiana.

Marc was one of those people who looked the same whatever age he reached. It was there in the structure of his face and the bright cheeky look in his bright blue eyes.

Fabiana smiled politely as he ushered her forward almost blinded by the photographers as their equipment flashed all around her. She stopped and paused for several minutes here and there, for the photographers, chatting to them, smiling, posing and signing a few autographs. The crowd loved her and she knew how to play them so well.

Fabiana was attired in a long black satin evening gown, her honey coloured skin in contrast. The dress draped elegantly from one shoulder. Her long dark hair was swept up in a bunch of curls that showed off her long neck and single bare shoulder to perfection. She wore the diamond drop earrings that Antonio had given her long ago and she stood tall in her gold high heel Manoli shoes and she held a small gold leather clutch evening bag.

Her eyes panned across the spectators with affection as they followed her. In an industry where most models were so terrified of losing their looks and denting their images, she didn't care. She had the style and charisma. The paparazzi just loved her.

Marc grinned engagingly at Fabiana as he stood by her watching her. A little pang of jealously went through him, he had fallen under her charm and would do anything for her.

Fabiana knew her new chauffeur had the hots for her and she did fancy him a lot. She knew she would have to make the moves. He was too polite to make any advances to her.

In less than forty eight hours' time she would be divorced from Tristan.

Antonio had come to her rescue again and engaged one of the top barristers in London to handle her divorce quickly and amicably. Once again she felt hurt and deluded with the World but Antonio had also come up with a plan regarding her having a child.

***

Fabiana slipped out of bed and tiptoed to the bathroom and looked at herself critically in the mirror; her face was still glowing from being pleasured by Marc the night before. She liked waking up next to him; it made her smile to remember the pleasure of the previous night. It was an uncomplicated relationship. Sex between them was always so good. He was young and energetic. She had also told him a little about her past.

She propped herself up on one elbow and looked at him and stroked his handsome face. His lips moved in a kiss against her hand, but he was still partially asleep. She wondered if in time he would stay with her and they would be in a similar situation, like Antonio's aunt in France had been with Ludo. She wondered how Ludo was and she must go and see him and Mrs Rutledge one of these days in England.

There was still no evidence of the scar on her face, though she often had dreams about the experimental surgery, which lasted for several month after Antonio had adopted her. The surgeon had said that her scarring would never come back, but sometimes she was afraid it might. She still had nightmares about the horrible man who had caused the fire and how she might have been scarred for life, if Antonio had not come to her aid.

Even though she was getting older she had not one wrinkle or line on her beautiful face. She had the complexion of a young woman in her early twenties, though no one really knew her exact age.

She showered and dried herself, dressed and sprayed herself with her favourite perfume … *L'Or de Torrente.*

Then she twisted her long hair into a neat French pleat and put on her make-up, with the skill she had learned from watching countless professionals at work on her face, from her basket of foundations, eye colours and lip-glosses. Then she checked herself for lines, but her smooth skin still looked ageless.

She went to her wardrobe and selected a black trouser suit, a cream silk shirt, black Jimmy Choo, medium heeled black leather ankle boots. She put her slim gold watch that Antonio had given her a long time ago, on her left wrist and a simple pearl choker necklace and pearl studs in her ears.

Fabiana wanted to look simple, but elegant. She knew she looked good, almost formidable and she would show the world what her husband was missing by divorcing her.

***

Fabiana spent most of the morning with her barrister in London and eventually everything was finalised. Tristan did not attend the meeting he was incommunicado. On his orders, his barrister stood in for him.

She signed all the papers and within four hours she was once more a free woman. Just before leaving her barrister's office he handed her a letter from Tristan, she stuffed it into her large black handbag and left the building. She would read the letter later on. In many ways she still had some feeling for Tristan, maybe they could be friends in the future.

The London paparazzi, as usual were hovering outside including some of the TV crews from different

TV stations all over the World waiting for Fabiana to appear.

Marc who had driven her to the High Courts in London in her new white Rolls Royce waited patiently by her side, whilst she spoke to some TV people and had her photo taken several times and then ushered her into her car and they drove away.

Two days later she had a phone call from Tristan asking her if she had read his letter and if they could still be friends. He told her he really did love her in his own way and asked for her forgiveness for the way he had treated her when they were married. He also told her, that he would always be by her side if she needed him. Perhaps one of these days they could get together and go for a meal on his next trip to London. She would phone him over the next couple of days and have a chap or maybe go out to lunch.

She did not bear malice because she knew that she would never be happy until she and Antonio were together once again. Everything happens for a reason she told herself.

It was also rumoured that she was giving up modelling and concentrating more on designing a new range of ladies' clothes for the 'over forties,' plus a new fragrance for older men and women.

CHAPTER FIFTEEN
FABIANA'S AWAKENING

She liked waking up next to Marc. It made her smile to remember the pleasure of the previous night. It was an uncomplicated relationship. Sex between them was always so good. He was young and energetic. They had been together now for one year since her divorce.

She propped herself up on one elbow and looked at him and stroked his face as she leaned into him in an intimate manner. Her lips were closed he could feel her breasts on his supple body and alive in his arms. She nibbled at his face and his mouth hesitantly, and then kissed him. His lips moved in a kiss against her hand, but he was still asleep or pretended to be.

"You know I'm offering you complete passion darling, with no strings attached." She said smilingly.

In Fabiana's glittering world of fashion and films, friends were harder to find than lovers and she did not want to lose him. She laughed nervously.

She knew that the only man she could ever really settle down with was Antonio. She also knew that one of these days he would come back into her life. But until then he would look after her because he still loved her so much.

She kissed Marc again, her soft and open lips moving back and forth, round and round, increasing the pressure, her tongue slipping into his mouth tenderly. Teasing and probing, promising passion, not an illusion.

Marc lifted her chin and her pulse quickened as he kissed her passionately.

CHAPTER SIXTEEN
ANTONIO RETURNS

Fabiana had a call from Antonio; he was staying in Switzerland at the Beau-Rivage Palace on the banks of Lake Geneva as usual.

He had arrived a week before without telling her. He wanted to meet her in the hotel dining room for lunch the next day. Her tickets were waiting at London Heathrow at the Swissair check-in counter.

As she entered the dining room of the famous hotel, the hum of conversation floated towards her.

She glanced around and nodded to several people who knew her by sight. Her face was famous on so many magazines and bill boards all over the World.

She was taken by the Head Waiter to Antonio's table where he was sitting by a window overlooking the banks of Lake Geneva.

It was a long time since she had seen him; she thought he looked rather tired.

Catching sight of her at the same time, Antonio got up in one smooth movement and began winding his way through the tables and chairs towards her.

Despite herself, she was struck how handsome he still looked in his early sixties. His tailor-made dark blue suit hugged his muscular frame like a glove. As he ducked clear of one of the low beams in the restaurant, a spotlight gleamed and his once very dark hair shone with natural silver highlights.

A flood of sexual awareness ran through her body. He was more handsome and sexy looking now that he was older, and he still walked in a lithe way, like a panther showing himself off to his mate.

She realised she wasn't the only one who'd noticed. Heads turned to follow his progress. Female eyes flickered with admiration and male eyes with envy.

Fabiana wanted him most of all, but he was her friend not his lover.

After all these years, she thought, he still had that magic power, her senses tingled. Her heart missed a beat. His thick hair was well cut and combed back, there were quite a few grey hairs each side of his temples, and somehow though, they made him look more attractive. She also noticed that he seemed to have lost some weight, but she put that down to his age and the vitality that he burnt up.

She felt a flutter in her stomach, she knew she was blushing and her head was pounding as the nearness of him sparked the memories she had kept hidden for several years.

He pushed his Ray Bans onto the top of his head and narrowed his eyes as he took in every detail of her. He still loved her so much and he wanted her in his arms. As usual she had come to him when everything was going wrong. He had asked her to come to Switzerland in order to help her through her emotional crisis and also because he missed her.

"Hello Fabiana you look wonderful, I have missed you all this time."

His voice was deep and full of passion for her. He put his hands on her shoulders and kissed her on each cheek. Then he pulled away from her slightly and looked at her with love in his eyes.

"I have missed you *cara mia.*"

His attractive voice with its Italian accent poured over her, she loved to hear him speak, it was so sexy and she knew he was not really aware of the effect he had on all women.

***

After their lunch they went up to his suite and he told her why he was in Switzerland.

He explained that just ten years ago he had his sperm put into a sperm bank whilst he was still healthy and active, just in case anything happened to him. He'd done it for several selfish reasons, one being in case she never married or she got divorced and he died unexpectedly, the main reason being though, was that he had found out that Tristan was gay and he knew that their marriage would not survive and he knew how much she wanted a child and he wanted her to have his.

He then told her that Tristan had told him he was bi-sexual but leaning more towards being gay and they had spoken of it before the marriage and he had promised not to tell her until the time was right.

"I can help you Fabiana, I want you to have a child by me. I have no male heir to follow me when I die. I have seen your medical records and your blood group is compatible with mine. I know you have no inherent diseases. You are perfect. I know you also want to have a child of your own, we are an ideal couple. The child or perhaps children in time will have everything they want; you and they will never go without."

Fabiana looked shocked for a few moments, he was right of course, she did want children or at least one child and she wanted his. He was the only man whom she really loved in her life.

She looked up at his face and knew that he really cared for her more than anything else in his life. That made it all the more right somehow. As she looked at him she realised that he was more handsome than ever, she still loved him and she did want a child of his.

But could she conceive after what had happened to her all those years ago she wondered? She knew that Antonio would have looked into that matter too.

Antonio continued.

"You remember Dr. Eduardo Martinez, he has for a long time owned a clinic in Lausanne, where he specializes in women who are not able to have children for certain reasons and many men have donated their sperm just in case they have an accident or die prematurely, they can then pass on part of their genetic heritage. My friend Eduardo also says that it may not work the first time because of what happened to you all those years ago, you might need some surgery. I have all the information in case anything should happen to me. He lives in Switzerland permanently now and has a thriving practice. We shall go and see him and perhaps start the treatment as soon as possible. Dr. Martinez will determine the time of ovulation and the day of the insemination. You will have a vaginal ultrasound for measurements and a blood or urine test at first and then he will decide when to inseminate you, with my sperm."

She was a little taken aback, but then she always obeyed Antonio and she knew Dr. Martinez very well, he had saved her life long ago and was an excellent gynaecologist.

"If you like, we could get married later and be a real family. That is something that I have wanted all my life. I do love you and I know you love me too. We are one and the same; we bonded the night I took you away from your mother and all that squalor. We were made for each other."

He paused whilst waiting for her answer and coughed and when he did so it felt that his chest would rip apart. So far only Doctor Martinez and his advocate in France, who was a close friend of his, knew just how bad his lung cancer was, the ripping sensation in his chest that was so frightening.

When he'd coughed up blood in the beginning, he had quickly flushed it down the wash hand basin when he was staying in Milan a few months before. He had immediately afterwards phoned his friend in Switzerland and booked a flight.

He was told by the specialist that he had a particularly aggressive type of cancer, both of his lungs were involved and perhaps his breastbone. The tumours were too far gone, surgery was out of the question and it was only a matter of time now. He did not want to tell Fabiana, he wanted to die quietly, everything was in order. He had very strong painkillers which helped him through the pain as well as the chemotherapy.

"Yes, you are right, I have never loved another man as I have loved you. You are my life." She said quietly and smiled lovingly at him.

He took her in his arms and held her tightly. He had missed her over the last six years or so. He was aging quickly now and dying of cancer, he didn't want to die on his own.

All his monetary affairs were in place with his advocates in France and another in London. He did not tell her yet why he was doing it. He was hoping every day that perhaps there could be some new drugs to prolong his life. Miracles can happen!

"As you know my aunt Elizabeth left me her château in her will, perhaps we could re-furbish the place and live there, I know how much you loved it when you stayed there. It would be the ideal home for our children and for us. Oh, by the way I have rented a suite for us here in the hotel and we can stay here until all your tests are finished and you conceive. Marriage will come later of course. Meantime I think you should enjoy your stay here for a couple of days or so, a little shopping perhaps before seeing the specialist!" He grinned at her, he suddenly felt young again.

Being there with Fabiana brought back memories with an intensity he had been unprepared for. He knew the veil between the present and the past was too thin; he needed her to spend the rest of his life with him or at least a few years.

Fabiana just nodded her head, as usual she trusted him and a child was something that she had wanted for a long time and having his sperm made things perfect in her mind.

She watched Antonio's face. It was dark-eyed with a strong jaw, black hair greying and receding a little from his high brow. She could read nothing in it. It was a face that would only give away exactly what its owner wished it to be.

Antonio knew that he would eventually have to tell Fabiana that he was dying of cancer, there was no hope, but in the meantime he must fly back to London to tie up certain things with his English solicitor, who already knew the situation.

When he was in Switzerland seeing his friend Dr. Eduardo Martinez he was diagnosed with the cancer, however, Dr, Martinez also told him that there was a certain new treatment that had not been passed yet which could possibly prolong his life but he would have to live in Switzerland for the trials. Antonio was glad that he had taken the doctor's advice ten years before to freeze some of his sperm at the Sperm Bank in Switzerland. In the meantime he had to get all of his affairs in order, before he had the painful task of telling Fabiana what was happening was dying in the meantime.

BOOK NINE
CHAPTER SEVENTEEN
EIGHTEEN MONTHS LATER

After several small operations and attempts at artificial insemination with Antonio's frozen sperm, Fabiana was now six and a half months pregnant with their son inside of her and Antonio was away in Paris on business again, leaving her in London.

Before he left, he arranged to spend some time at Château Elizabeth giving the place a face lift before her baby was born. He felt so young again and he was having respite from the cancer, but for how long he didn't know, he had also gained some weight, which was a good sign

***

Some resemblance of reality was returning to her, the shock of what had happened had cleared her brain of the effects of the unaccustomed glass of alcohol that she had drunk when she heard about Antonio's car crash from Dr. Martinez over the telephone, but she still felt nauseous.

She had been informed by his friend Doctor Martinez who was also in Paris but not in the car with him at the time, that Antonio had been involved in a car crash south east of Paris in a tunnel. He was in a coma in Pitie-Salpetriere Hospital.

Also she was afraid that the shock might endanger her baby she was carrying.

Dr. Martinez had phoned her and said he would be waiting for her at Charles de Gaulle airport.

Doctor Martinez saw her coming through the French barrier and smiled gently. He thought she looked as beautiful as ever as he took her hand luggage and also her right arm.

"I have my chauffeur waiting outside perhaps you would like to go straight to the hospital first. I will tell you what happened to Antonio on the way. By the way, I have booked you in a hotel near the hospital."

The thought of Antonio dying wasn't real to her. How could she believe it?

She started trembling as the doctor told her what had happened, but she held her tears back as much as possible.

"Antonio told me he was coming back from Switzerland from the clinic to meet you in Paris, but I'm afraid to tell you that his lung cancer which over the last two years now, is an unusual aggressive type. He has kept it from you and over the years he has had chemotherapy in Switzerland, but I'm afraid that he will really not get any benefit from it anymore. He of course knows this and I have a terrible feeling that he might even have crashed his car on purpose. "

The doctor paused for a moment.

"Antonio is a very proud man as you know and he kept most of his illness from you. Fortunately when he had the tests for the sperm bank all those years ago there was nothing wrong with him at all. You don't have to worry for your unborn child. You do know that your child is a boy and will take the surname of Donnetti. This is a request of Antonio's."

Fabiana looked at the doctor, she'd had no idea about how bad Antonio's illness was and wondered if he would have eventually told her. She was faint with grief.

When Fabiana and Doctor Martinez they arrived at the hospital they were accompanied by a nurse to Antonio's private ward.

When she saw him she wanted to kick out at something, yell at him to wake him up. It wasn't fair she screamed in her head. It just wasn't fair.

The doctors were keeping him alive on a life-support machine. At least perhaps there was hope for him. She couldn't imagine what it would have been like if he had died before she arrived and to see him in a Paris morgue and have to identify his body.

"I'll be back this afternoon." She told the doctor in charge.

***

Doctor Martinez took her back to the hotel and at 4pm they returned back to the hospital.

"May I see him now?" She asked the doctor and this time she went to the room alone.

The nurses were still there and stepped aside so she could approach Antonio's bed. She stood looking down at him, his eyes were closed and she touched his cheek gently. The tubes from the respirator nearly covered his face and she saw the bandage around his head and wondered how much damage the accident had actually caused.

She felt a tenderness and love for him that was just as strong as anyone saw in a love story or film. But she knew that she hadn't shown that love openly to him for a long time.

"I love you so much Antonio. I have always loved you. I am sorry if I hurt you in the past."

She whispered. "You need to wake up soon please, my darling."

There was no sign of life from the bed, and the nurses looked discreetly away. It was hard for them to watch the beautiful woman; there was so much pain in her eyes.

Fabiana bent to kiss Antonio's left cheek and remembered the familiar softness of his skin. Even all these years later, that hadn't changed. His long black hair, tinged with a lot of grey now, had been brushed off his face and fanned out behind him on the pillow.

Fabiana bent over the bed and kissed him and tried to take him in her arms. She wanted to tell him how much she loved him. How she had hurt him in the past, but he had always been there, now she was there to hold him.

She knew there was no hope that he would come back to her. She was told that his head injuries were too severe, even if he did recover he would be severely brain damaged and she knew he would not want to live like that.

She wanted to remember him as the handsome man that she would have finally married and lived with happily for ever after, but it was not to be so.

She looked up at the machine that was keeping him alive and suddenly there was nothing except a flat line that was whining and then no noise at all.

Her eyes welled up with tears; she knew he was finally at rest.

His hospital doctor and Doctor Martinez came forward and Fabiana looked up at them.

They both shook their heads.

"I'm sorry Madame we can do no more for him." Said the French doctor.

Dr. Martinez took Fabiana in his arms and said quietly.

"You know he would never have wanted to live as a dying man, he was such a vital man. He has gone to God now, but he will always be there for you, wherever you are and you **are** carrying his child. "

She turned in a dignified manner and walked away. She would grieve quietly in her own time. Everything that Antonio owned was to be hers, but in her dreams she wanted only him.

EPILOGUE

The funeral was over and she'd seen the various advocates regarding Antonio's fortune. He'd bequeathed to her, $7.5billion along with all of his various estates and investments all over the World, including the Donnetti business, Unbeknown to her he had been the son of a drugs baron and inherited the fortune his late father had accumulated and invested before his parents were in a car accident all those years ago.

A very large amount of money was left to Dr. Eduardo Martinez to extend his hospital in Switzerland and for more research for women from around the World who had difficulty in conceiving and could have free treatment. Dr. Martinez also intended to send a substantial amount of money to the old hospital in Bogotá to improve the lives of some of the women in the area.

***

Shortly after Antonio's funeral, Fabiana, who was now seven months pregnant, decided to return to Lyon where she would have her baby and Marc would drive her over in her new Jaguar. She wanted to see what needed to be done to Château Elizabeth before finally moving in.

Marc and Fabiana gazed through the windscreen at the 15th century Château. The high black wrought iron gates in front of the driveway were already open for them.

They drove slowly up to the front door, letting the engine idle for a while and then she got out fumbling for the house keys. It was to be her home now, a 20 thousand acre estate, indoor and outdoor swimming pools, elegant terraces, rolling lawns down to a river.

She noticed the grounds were in pristine condition and she wondered who was in charge of them.

She'd been given to understand that the place was empty. She also noticed that the rambling roses on the surrounding walls had obviously been pruned not long ago and wondered who was looking after her new home and grounds.

The air was slightly cold that spring morning and seared through her lungs as she paused at the doorstep, trying to analyse her feelings, then she turned the key, pushed the door open and stepped inside. The house was warm; obviously someone had the central heating set low.

The inside was rather shabby but the house seemed very clean, the smooth brick built floor of the entrance had a soft patina; the chandeliers were sparkling, however a second glance showed fading paint and scuffed marks on the skirting boards. Most of the furniture needed to be discarded or renovated. She remembered how it had been when Antonio's aunt was living there.

She walked slowly through the first floor and looked up at the beautiful 15th century oak beams, kindling memories as she did so when she had last been there with Antonio a year before when they were looking over the château deciding on how they would redecorate and bring it back to life again.

The formal dining room was large and pleasant and the long mahogany dining table was shining, someone had polished it lovingly.

There were three large portraits on the wall in the hallway, one of Antonio's mother the other of his deceased aunt and Antonio when he was a small boy.

"This will be your future home where I will bring you up. Your father would have liked that." She murmured to the child inside of her. She felt him moving as if he knew that this would be his new home.

Slowly she walked up the wide wooden stairway looking in the romantic bedrooms with their four-poster beds and lace covers on them. She noticed that two bedrooms had been cleaned and were ready for her. But she could see no one around and wondered who could have done it.

When she had finished the investigation of her new home, she went back down into the kitchen.

She heard male voices. There were two men sitting at the long wooden refractory kitchen table drinking coffee and they both seemed to be very much at home.

One was Marc her chauffeur and another man.

She stopped at the doorway and somehow knew that she had seen him before, but it was a long time ago. The tall thin man was speaking to Marc in accented English and he stood up to greet her. He was tall and he had blue eyes very similar to her own. His hair that was once dark was greying at the sides and quite long, pulled back into a ponytail. His head was slightly at one side. Perhaps he'd been in a fight many years ago or had an accident she thought.

She stared at him for several minutes trying to recall where she knew him from.

"Hello, my little Maria, it's been a long, long time."

He spoke in Spanish to her and suddenly she knew, but she couldn't believe it, the last time she'd seen him was when she was in her very early teens. He was her older brother Carlos whom she thought had been killed many years ago, or so her late mother had told her and he got up from the table and took her in his arms and they both laughed and cried at the same time.

Marc watched them and felt a lump in his throat. He'd known about Carlos in a letter that Antonio had sent to him sometime after he had taken the job of chauffeuring and being a bodyguard to Fabiana. He had given a promise to Antonio not to tell her as Antonio had wanted to surprise her himself when they finally moved into the château. Antonio, in his wisdom had known that she would need someone to look after her when he had gone and he had given Marc instructions to try and trace the rest of her family when the time came. Antonio also knew that history would repeat itself and Fabiana would end up living in France one day.

She too would have her lover Marc and her brother to look after her and her son. Tristan would remain a good friend despite their previous difficulties and when the time was right she would ask him to be the godfather to Antonio's son.

Her smart phone suddenly rang out and she looked at the screen and clicked it off. Simon was obviously very keen to contact her again. She knew he would keep calling her until she answered, but she decided that she wouldn't, he had done the same thing to her in the past. She would now do it to him. He was probably only after her money. Antonio had warned her about Simon when they were in Switzerland discussing their future. She no longer needed Simon anyway.

The End

Lightning Source UK Ltd.
Milton Keynes UK
UKHW042327130519
342594UK00001B/10/P